KEWEENAW FAITH

BRIAN K. HOLMES

WESTBOW
P R E S S®
A DIVISION OF THOMAS NELSON
& ZONDERVAN

WestBow Press books may be ordered through booksellers or by contacting:

WestBow Press
A Division of Thomas Nelson & Zondervan
1663 Liberty Drive
Bloomington, IN 47403
www.westbowpress.com
1 (866) 928-1240

ISBN: 978-1-9736-4322-7 (sc)
ISBN: 978-1-9736-4321-0 (e)

Library of Congress Control Number: 2018912485

Print information available on the last page.

WestBow Press rev. date: 11/09/2018

DEDICATION PAGE

FOR PASTORS: MARK E. SPAW
AND PASTOR LINDA LIVING HAWLEY
(MY SPIRITUAL MENTORS)

POEM

HOPE IS A LADDER; HOPE IS A TEACHER
HOPE IS THE VISION YOU HAVE FOR THE FUTURE
HOPE IS THE PEACE YOU HAVE IN YOUR HEART
HOPE IS A LONG ROAD HOME

FAITH IS THE PLACE AT THE TOP OF THE LADDER
FAITH IS THE LESSON PLANNED FOR TOMORROW
FAITH IS THE STRENGTH TO LIFT YOU ABOVE
FAITH LET'S YOU KNOW THERE'S A HOME

GRACE IS THE FEELING
YOU'VE CLIMBED THE HIGH MOUNTAIN
GRACE IS THE JOY THAT COMES FROM WITHIN
GRACE IS THE KNOWING YOUR FUTURE IS NOW
GRACE IS THE PALM OF HIS HAND.

                                    BRIAN K. HOMES

UPPER AND LOWER PENINSULAS

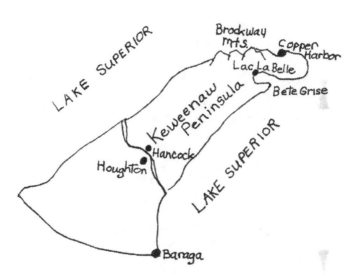

KEWEENAW PENINSULA

ACKNOWLEDGEMENT

Just a word of thanks to the small but ever growing group of the Keweenaw Series fan club who have jumped on board the Johnny Hendricks experience with me.

You're feedback and suggestions are what have brought us this far. I am extremely grateful.

BKH

PROLOGUE

A pall hangs over the close knit City of Hancock in Michigan's Upper Peninsula as many lives are affected by the horrific car crash caused by a snowy white out along the coast of Lake Superior in the Keweenaw. Physical paralysis and despair have brought Johnny to his knees at this low point in his life.

CHAPTER 1

Keith Koski was born somewhere between Psychedelia and the Bossa Nova and grew up amidst the confusion of a transitioning world. This world included his father Norm, a hard working Polish American patriot and veteran of the Korean Conflict with solid roots in the Catholic Church and the Democrat Party. He was a Kennedy progressive and a hold on to your hat conservative in the years after the political assassinations of the 60's. As the world he knew spun out of control, he and his wife Barbara brought Keith into the world. Barbara typified the late twentieth century house wife with a neat and tidy home and a part time job selling cosmetics to local beauty parlors. Her mother, Grandma Phyllis, or Buscha as the family called her, had lost her husband Ray long before Keith could remember. She had always been part of his world and slept in the only downstairs bedroom in this happy home.

Sundays and Holidays were special in the Koski household because it meant hours of family time and his mom and grandma always enjoyed it when dad wasn't working. Even as a young boy, Sunday morning was fun because everybody at Mass always made him feel special, and of course they always went out for lunch after church. Those were the days of chicken dinners and mashed potatoes smothered in rich yellow gravy. He often wondered what it would be like having a brother or sister to pal around with, but after considering the possibility, he mostly liked being the center of attention.

Growing up on the west side of Grand Rapids had a certain structure to it. Life was formed around dad's job, and the family, and the ribbon wrapped around their lives was the church. As a child the significance of this buffer against the outside world meant little to him, but as his experiences expanded there was an inner pride; a sense that Polish/American Catholics were the chosen ones.

Those who lived on the east side of the Grand River were mostly of Dutch extraction, and unfortunately embraced the same ethnic arrogance as their Polish counterparts. Sprinkled in amongst the rest of the population was a smaller area of African-Americans and Latinos which created a cosmopolitan soup for Keith to digest. This dichotomy of souls became evident as Keith entered West Catholic High School and became a member of the football team. Although it wasn't obvious at the time, the attitudes a defensive lineman on the 'Falcons' and prejudices of the older generations held a profound effect on the teenagers of the day, but no one thought much about it.

It wasn't until Keith graduated from West Catholic and entered Aquinas College that he was forced to face the real world. The west side of the Grand River was only an island in a sea of possibilities, and the transition was difficult at first. Keith would rush back across the river after his classes to what was comfortable. No one noticed; no one cared. That all changed the day he spotted a pretty young co-ed sitting on a bench in front of the Science Building with her head held back toward the sun catching some rays. Her blond hair pulled back into a pony tail glistened against the clear blue sky. Keith noticing this young beauty, threw his books in the back seat of his car and walked across the parking lot drawn like a moth to a flame. No longer in control of his body he circled her once and sat down on a bench twenty feet to her right. He wanted to meet her but didn't want to appear like a stalker. The fear that she might get up and leave, never to be seen again, caused panic in his heart so he made the next move.

"Excuse me," he said, slowly approaching the other end of her bench. "Is this seat taken?" Feeling like an idiot for even saying something so stupid, he quickly looked in the other direction.

"Were you talking to me?" She asked, shading her eyes with her hand.

"Yes," said Keith, abruptly putting his brain on pause.

"Are you a student here?" She inquired in a detached manner. After all, he was the one who interrupted her sunshine.

"Yeah, my first term," he responded, matching her dispassion word for word.

"I'm Mary," she continued, "Mary Vander Meer. I'm a freshman," she added, her face opening up in a smile.

"Are you from Grand Rapids?" Keith asked, sliding a little closer as if he was hard of hearing.

"Rockford," she responded, "but I've spent most of my life here. We moved when I was in high school."

"It must've been tough making all new friends," Keith said sympathetically.

"Where are you from?" She asked not responding to his assumption.

"The west side; West Catholic High," he said filling in the blanks.

"We're not anything," she said out of nowhere, wondering why she even said it.

"You must be something. Everybody's something," he grinned. "With a name like Vander Meer, I'm guessing you're not of Polish descent."

"You can probably toss out Irish and Italian too," she said facetiously.

"I'm beginning to think your ancestors might have jumped off the boat from Amsterdam," he deduced.

"Who would've thought that I'd run into a Polish genius right her in my own home town."

"Stranger things have happened," he posed.

"Not to me," she countered.

"Anyway, I'm Keith Koski; Polish yes, genius no."

"Honesty is better than genius," she laughed. "Genius is over rated."

"What's your major?" Keith asked earnestly.

"Orthopedic nursing," Mary responded.

"What about you?" She asked, quickly brushing a long blond hair from her face.

"General Business, I had to pick something," he said.

Colleges were the same across the country. Whether you knew your future or not, indifference was not an option.

"I've gotta run," she said looking at her watch. "I've got a two o'clock over in the science lab." She stood collecting her books.

Before Keith could even object or delay her departure, she was gone. *That was nice*, he thought, suddenly feeling in no particular hurry. *Maybe she'll be here after my freshman Trig class on Wednesday*, he mused walking slowly towards his car.

"Mary," Professor Peterson repeated, staring at the young lady with a scalpel in one hand and a frog in the other. "Once again can you explain to the rest of the class where we start the incision on our small friend here for an abdominal inspection?"

The sound of the professor's voice was a million miles away as she continued to personally chastise herself for the opportunity she had just squandered. She just froze again. It had been three years, and she hadn't had an intelligent conversation with a boy her own age since the accident.

"Well, I guess Mary's not with us today," Peterson said. "Do you have any thoughts on the subject Sophia?" He said pointing to a girl in the back of the lab.

CHAPTER 2

Mary was one of the two survivors of a car vs. deer collision in her junior year of high school. Her best friend Amy, and her boy friend Bill, crashed through the windshield on the passenger side and were gone. The driver Johnny managed to survive but was hospitalized and in a coma. Mary without as much as a scratch was just lost. She and her folks had attended Bill's funeral, but it was as if she was looking down from above. Her high school friends tried to hug her and touch her, but she wasn't there. Bill's mother was inconsolable and his dad looked back at Mary from the front pew at the funeral and sadly whispered, "I'm so sorry."

During the last prayer, Mary ran up the aisle followed by her parents, wishing she was lying next to Bill.

Amy's funeral was the following day. Mary's mom called Amy's mother and told her that Mary wasn't well enough to attend. Amy's mother said she understood, and would try and visit Mary very soon, but she never did.

A few weeks later her dad suggested a fresh start might be helpful, and by Christmas their house was up for sale. A nice ranch house north of Grand Rapids near the Rogue River in Rockford was available, and because the driving distance to his work was about the same, a deal was struck.

Mary was too traumatized to immediately start back to high school in a new city so her mom home schooled her while she had stress counseling twice a week.

The first few months were brutally depressing. The freezing temperatures and the lake effect snow squalls from nearby Lake Michigan kept her home bound most of the time. Her only companion was Corky, her cocker spaniel, and most of the time Corky's soft blond fur soaked up her tears.

April brought in moderating temperatures, and she and Corky would take daily walks down to Peppler Park on the Rogue River in downtown Rockford. The rushing water from the snow melt upstream crashed into the top of the dam blowing a spray of mist in the air as she and her dog sat on a bench at the riverside park.

In May the trees all blossomed and the two would walk the paths on both sides of the river watching nature fulfill its promise. These were much better days for her as her parents saw a big improvement in her demeanor. On one of her walks she found a 'now hiring' sign on a window in a card shop down on Main Street. She and Corky entered the shop, and after a short conversation she was hired on the spot.

Outside of her work she seemed to exist in a vacuum that no one could penetrate. Her folks tried everything to break the bubble and release their daughter back into the world of the present. She called Johnny Hendricks, the driver in the accident, but always hung up when someone answered the phone. Her counselor advised that it might be a helpful for her to enter Rockford High School for her senior year. The challenge of trying to fit back into the real world might be the spark she needed to go on with her life in a positive way.

The day after Labor Day, Mary stood on the street corner waiting for her school bus. She was one of the few seniors who didn't drive herself to school, but was oblivious to the stigmatism her fellow seniors would place on her for riding a bus with underclassmen.

"Is this seat taken?" She asked an obvious under classman.

The younger girl slid over by the window allowing Mary to sit down.

"You're new here," the seatmate said as a statement of fact. "How'd you know?" Mary asked.

"I've been riding this same bus since ninth grade and I've never seen you before. My name's Bella."

"That's a very pretty name," Mary responded, "My name's Mary."

"It may be very pretty to you, but all of the Tinkerbelle's in eleventh grade call me 'Belly' cause I'm little over weight." "That can't make you feel very good," said Mary.

"Naw, it's no big thing," Bella said dismissing the obvious affronts. "All of the Delveccios on my father's side are big boned so it's just a family thing."

Bella, sometimes called 'chatterbox' by her mom and dad, was a people person with an outgoing personality. She was a smaller version of her mom Flo, and that was fine by her.

"Do you have a best friend?" Mary asked.

"Not a very best friend," Bella admitted, "I just kind of hang out with the gang."

"Well that's good, because I don't have any friends, except for my dog Corky."

"You've got a dog?" Bella asked so loud that everyone on the bus turned and looked at her.

"Just a little one," said Mary noticing the attention her seat mate had drawn to them.

"Lucky," said Bella with envy. "I'll bet he's nice," she added. "Is it a boy dog?"

"Yeah," she added, happy to praise her four legged friend.

"Well, here we go," said Bella collecting her books preparing to exit the bus in front of the High School.

The imposing red brick pillars protecting the main entrance made Mary wonder if she was ready to get back into the real world.

Bella waved at friends as they entered the building.

"Come on," she said taking Mary's arm, "I'll show you where the office is."

Bella ushered her to the door and then disappeared down the hall. The clamor throughout the building made Mary want to run for the exit, but she had promised her parents and councilor she would give it a fair shake.

"May I help you?" asked a rather large woman with long shapeless curls hanging on either side of a dour face. Her right hand forefinger pushed a pair of nondescript glasses farther up her pug nose.

"I'm Mary Vander Meer," she said as confidently as she could. "I'm transferring from a home school program to finish my senior year here at Rockford High."

The office staffer whose plain white blouse was bedecked with a small black pin with the name 'Jan' embossed on it, pushed her wheeled office chair straight back, scooped up a form from a table, and glided effortlessly back to Mary in what seemed like a singular move.

"Fill out this form and have your parent or guardian sign it and return it tomorrow morning. Sharon," she shouted to a younger office staffer to her left. "Take this young lady to Ms. Bacon in 105 for her first hour. May I help you?" She asked the boy standing behind Mary.

School hadn't changed much since she had moved. Lots

of high energy teenagers trying to fit in and adapt to a new situation similar but somehow different from their last year.

"You must be Mary Vander Meer," said a thirty-something bespectacled woman with a pleasant smile. "Find an available seat at one of the tables, and we'll get started."

Mary went to the second row and sat down next to a girl who looked up and smiled at her.

"Hi, I'm Mindy, welcome," she whispered.

"I'm Mary," echoed the new student.

And so it began, from History in the first hour, to College Prep Trig in the sixth, Mary ran the gauntlet of her first day at Rockford High School, smiling, being polite, and wishing she was anywhere else.

When she finally plopped down next to Bella for the ride home, she began weeping.

"I can't do this," she said quietly, "It just hurts too much."

"What happened?" Bella asked. "Were they hateful to you?"

"No," Mary sniffled. "They were all very nice, but," she paused unable to finish her thought.

‎ ‎

"Mary came down with something," her mother told the school office the following morning.

Sitting in her room with Corky staring at the wall was all she could handle for the next few days.

"There's some one here to see you," her mother yelled up the stairs.

No response.

"She says her name is Bella. She says she wants to meet Corky."

Mary immediately did a quick perusal of her bed room,

slid some papers and magazines under the bed, brushed her hair and sat back down on the bed as if nothing had happened.

"Hi Corky," Bella said, quietly entering the bedroom.

Corky shriveled up his nose and yipped at Bella.

"He won't bite," Mary said as she made room for Bella on the side of the bed.

Bella scratched the young cocker spaniel's ears as the dog tried to climb into her lap.

"How did you find me?" Mary asked.

"My mom called the school office, and they said you were sick or something."

"Well, I was kinda," said Mary watching Corky trying to climb up Bella to lick her face.

"I thought maybe it was me," Bella said sullenly, as if this wasn't the first time she had created problems in other people's lives.

"It's just something silly," Mary said looking at the wall.

"Did somebody say something at school?" Bella asked, hoping to get to the bottom of this, now that she realized she wasn't the cause.

"No," Mary answered. "How's school going?" She asked changing the subject.

"Okay, I guess. The same kids who were a pain last year are at it again," she said petting Corky. "I even lost a few pounds over the summer, but Roger Burns just won't let up. I talked to the councilor, but he says I'm just too sensitive. I'm just sick of it," she said in exasperation.

"Would you like to go for a walk?" Mary asked sliding off the edge of the bed.

"Can we take Corky?" Bella asked.

"If you want to, but he has to be on a leash, okay?"

"Deal," said Bella rushing down the upstairs hallway with Corky nipping at her heels.

"Come on, I'll show you where I live," said Bella turning the corner. "I told my mom all about you the first day we met, and she said that you sounded very nice. I don't have many friends because I'm so heavy," she rambled on. Bella took a few more steps and stopped. "Maybe we could be friends, or something," she said lowering her head.

"I'd like that a lot." Mary said watching Bella's face broaden into a grin.

"It smells like my mom made cookies," Bella said entering her house. "But," she said raising her finger, "I can only have one."

"Welcome," said Flo Delveccio wiping her hands on a well worn apron, "you must be Mary."

The warmth of her smile and out stretched hands was more inviting than the aroma of chocolate chip cookies.

"Bella's told us all about you. I sure hope you're feeling better. The school office said you were sick," she added with real concern.

"I'm feeling much better," said Mary. "I think maybe it was just nerves."

"Do you like chocolate chip cookies?" Mrs. Delveccio asked, "Bella seems to live on them."

The conversation drifted to where Mary had come from and things to see and do in and around the Rockford area. When Joe Delveccio came through the garage door with lunch pail in hand, Mary saw an opportunity to take Corky and head back home to her safe place.

CHAPTER 3

On Monday morning Mary and Bella exited the bus in front of the high school.

"Looking kind of svelte Belly; that new dress makes you look like a pencil," quipped Roger surrounded by friends as the two girls walked toward the school.

"Yeah," added Raymond, "a short fat pencil with a big eraser in the middle."

Bella rolled her eyes and kept walking, but Mary stopped.

"I'm sorry," she said loudly, walking up to the group of bullies. "Is there something I can do to help elevate your lives?"

Everyone within twenty feet of the challenge stopped what they were doing. No one knew this new girl, and after all, Roger was the point guard on the varsity basketball team.

"Nobody's talking to you," he snapped back at Mary.

"What are you and all your buddies going to do to us?" Mary responded raising her voice another notch so that everyone in the area could hear her.

The boys stepped back wishing they had picked a better spot. Besides, who was this new girl and who did she think she was. Roger made a rude gesture and said, "Forget you," slugging one of his buddies on the shoulder. They turned and strode confidently towards the school.

Bella looked around to see if anyone else was going to attack them, but everyone was looking at Mary. No one had ever stood up to the sports jocks before, and they were all smiling, although not to Roger's face.

"Come on Bella," said Mary marching toward the principal's office, "this is going to stop right now."

"We would like to speak to Mr. Sherman," directed Mary at a rather timid Jan sitting quietly behind her desk.

"You girls should be on your way to class," Jan menaced, looking straight at Mary.

"Is he in his office?" Mary countered not to be detoured.

An uncomfortable moment of silence followed.

"Tell Mr. Sherman that Mary Vander Meer and Bella Delveccio would like to meet with him concerning the bullying he allows in this public school."

The two girls turned and pushed their way through the group of gawking students jamming the office door.

"We're in for it now," Bella said to Mary as they headed for their first hour classes.

Twenty minutes later, Ms. Bacon was interrupted by a knock on her classroom door, and stepped into the hallway. Two minutes after that she re-entered the room, walked up to Mary and whispered, "Mr. Sherman will see you in his office. Bring your books."

Bella was already seated across from Jan as Mary entered the office. There were only the tapping sounds of Sharon's fingers on her keyboard as Bella looked into the eyes of her co-conspirator. At exactly 8:30a.m. Jan, with the voice of a hangman, said, "You may go in now."

Mr. Sherman, seated at his desk, looked up from a stack

of papers and with an engaging smile said, "Come in and sit down ladies."

Mr. Sherman studied another document, set down his pen and said, "Now what's this all about."

Mary and Bella both started talking at the same time.

Mary said, "This kind of behavior is unacceptable anywhere, especially in a high school."

Bella's opinion was that maybe it wasn't so bad.

Mr. Sherman sat back clicking his pen. "Tell me exactly what happened," he said like a presiding judge.

"Well…" Bella started.

"We had just exited the bus and were walking toward the building when Roger Burns and his friend made some derisive remarks directed at Bella," Mary said admonishingly.

"What did Roger say Bella?" The principal asked.

"Oh, just the usual," Bella quietly replied looking down at her hands.

"Roger said she looked like a pencil, and then his buddy added; a short fat pencil that was fat in the middle. They call her Belly."

"Is that right?" asked the principal.

"It's been a lot worse. They just won't leave me alone. I don't know why, I don't even know them."

"Do you have anything to add?" He asked Mary.

Mary feeling the helplessness in her new friend's voice took Bella's hand and shook her head.

"I will deal with this personally," Mr. Sherman said, "but you must promise me that if anyone of these boys harasses either of you in any way, you will contact me immediately."

Both girls nodded their heads and were dismissed. They slowly walked together down the hall until the second hour bell sounded. By lunch period the entire high school was abuzz with rumors and possibilities. Everyone stared at Mary when she entered the cafeteria and once again she was angry about a situation she hadn't started but seemed to be in the middle of. She bought a carton of milk and an apple and sat down at an empty table hoping no one would join her.

"Hi," said a girl she'd never seen before, dropping her tray and a big rag purse on the table right across from Mary. "I guess you're the new bombshell that dropped on Rockford High this morning. My name's Mara. We just moved from upstate New York, and I'm kind of new here too. It looks like you've found out that this isn't the friendliest place on the planet," she added.

If great looks and athletic ability were two attributes for drawing you into the inner circle of popularity, it was obvious that Mara wouldn't be joining the 'in-crowd' any time soon.

"You want some chips?" She asked Mary who was quartering her apple on a paper plate.

Mary responded to the offer by shaking her head without looking across the table.

"I'm sorry if it's been a rough morning," Mara said. "I'll be quiet if you need your space. It's just that I hate to see somebody eating alone. I've been doing it for a week now."

Mary looked up into a pair of sad eyes and suddenly realized how rude she had been to someone who obviously disliked this place as much as she did.

"I'm sorry," Mary said opening up to Mara. "I think you're right about the bombshell. It doesn't look like I'll be a candidate for Homecoming Queen either," she paused, "but I guess I'll get over it."

"Senior?" Mara asked opening a wrapped tuna salad sandwich trying to pick out the celery chunks.

"Yeah" Mary responded, "but it's my first year at Rockford. I transferred from another school; it's a long story."

"I saw you and your friend taking on the bad guys out side school this morning. I thought you were incredible," Mara said in an aroused tone. "You had those turkeys on the run in front of everybody. That made my whole day."

"I'm sorry, but you just can't treat people that way. It's just not right. Besides, Bella is my new friend," Mary said stubbornly.

"Is that her name?" Mara asked. "I think that's her coming this way."

Mary turned to spot her new compatriot heading towards their table with a small pepperoni pizza balanced on top of her books.

Bella slid the pizza on to the table and immediately ripped a slice from the pie and stuffed it in her mouth. Laughing and choking at the same time she said, "We're either the most popular or most unpopular two people in the school, depending on who you talk to," she said smiling at Mara.

"Come on," Mary said. "It can't really be that big of deal."

"I think every jock in school has jumped on Roger for letting a girl, I mean two girls get in his face. Believe me he's the laughing stock of Rockford, maybe the whole county."

Just then Roger and his entourage sauntered into the cafeteria, and spotting Mary, sat down at the table right behind her. The three girls stopped talking and waited for whatever came next. A moment later, a grape flew over Bella's head and landed on their table. Mary stood up, turned to face Roger, and asked with authority, "Why did you throw that?" She looked straight at Roger.

"Throw what?" Roger asked feigning a false sense of innocence.

"Roger," Mary said patiently, "I don't know why you and

your friends have decided to single out Bella and me, but this behavior is going to stop. Do you understand?"

"Do you understand?" mimicked one of Roger's posse in a falsetto voice, and all the boys laughed.

Mary looked around the cafeteria and nobody else was laughing. A cafeteria monitor was making a phone call, but silence prevailed around the big room. One by one the boys noisily pushed back their chairs and slowly walked past Mary's table while exiting the cafeteria. The last boy flipped another grape on the girl's table as he passed by. The silence was broken by an immediate and resounding round of applause, and the legend of Mary and Bella continued to grow.

At the beginning of fifth hour, Mary was once again summoned to the office. This time Jan just nodded towards the principal's door.

"Sit down Mary," Mr. Sherman said sympathetically.

The look in Mary's eyes told the principal that there would be no apology forthcoming or any regrets in her actions. Mary was on a mission and her feelings seemed irreversible.

Sitting very primly she said, "I think I owe you an explanation for my actions in the lunch room. Almost a year ago, eleven months ago to be exact, I was on a double date with my boy friend Bill, and best friend Amy and her date. It was dark and a deer ran in front of our car. Johnny, Amy's boyfriend, was driving and hit the deer broadside. We slid into a ditch and Amy in the front seat, crashed through the windshield and died instantly. Bill, in the backseat flew over Amy and broke his neck. Johnny hit the steering wheel and was knocked unconscious. I bounced off the back of the front seat and barely got a scratch." Void of emotion, Mary paused for a moment to collect her thoughts. "In an instant, two of the people I loved the most were gone, and I was left behind; no goodbyes, no hugs, no nothing," she stared past Mr. Sherman who was speechless. "I won't tell you the amount of therapy or self recrimination I have gone through to get where I am now. Not a day goes by that I don't relive that horrible moment and I have nightmares every night. In eleventh grade a best friend and a boyfriend are the closest people in your lives, and to lose them both in an instant…"

"Mary…" Mr. Sherman interrupted.

"No, wait," she cut in. "This is what I came to say." Mary stiffened her back. "Bella Delveccio is my best friend. I met her a week ago riding the bus on my first day of school. She was alone and told me that she was being bullied by this group of guys. She had no one to turn to. It was suggested that she was thin-skinned and should get over it. Mr. Sherman I have already lost one best friend and I will not allow a group of bullies to destroy Bella's life. Until you make this place safe for everyone, you will probably see me again. I've got to go home now. I'm not feeling very well. Can you please call my mother and have her pick me up?"

Mary rose quietly and turned to the open door. As she entered the outer office, Roger and his friends were sitting across from Jan waiting to see Mr. Sherman. Two of the boys had tears in their eyes; they had heard the whole thing. Mr. Sherman followed Mary from his office.

"Jan, will you please call Mrs. Vander Meer and see if she can pick Mary up." He looked over at the five boys who all wished they were somewhere else.

☾☽

"Where'd you go?" asked Bella later that evening. "I heard you got called back down to the office."

Mary was lying on her bed scratching Corky's ears. "Yeah Sherman the peace maker was at it again," she joked making light of the tense situation.

"Word has it the Rockford Five were expelled for three days." Bella said snickering.

"I don't know if that's the answer, but it's a start."

"Are you going back tomorrow?"

"I don't think so. I can't stand the notoriety. I just want to be left alone, you know what I mean?"

"I'm sorry I got you into this mess," Bella said quietly. "It didn't have nothin to do with you," she sad sadly.

"Bella it has to do with everybody. No one should be treated that way. It still makes me angry to think that a group of kids can get away with that."

"Well I'll call you tomorrow and let you know what's happening," Bella said, "Have a great evening."

Two hours later the phone rang again and Mary caught it on the second ring.

"Hello," she said.

"Could I please speak to Mary," an unknown voice said.

"May I ask who is calling?"

"Please don't hang up Mary. This is Roger Burns."

"Give me one good reason why I should talk to you."

"Because we all heard what you said to Mr. Sherman," he said emotionally, "and it broke my heart."

"Roger you haven't got a heart. You and your friends are a bunch of bullies."

"Go ahead, we all deserve it, but what you said in the office was the saddest thing I've ever heard."

There was silence on Mary's end of the line, and Roger thought that maybe she had hung up.

"How did you get my number?" Mary asked changing the subject.

"Bella."

"No way would she give you my number," she spat back.

"After Mr. Sherman expelled us for three days, I asked him if he would give me Bella's number so that I could apologize. I started this so I am responsible. He told me he would contact the Delveccios, but it was up to them."

"Mr. Delveccio called me an hour ago and he was really mad. Believe me it was pretty scary."

"What did he say?" Mary asked showing signs of interest.

"I won't repeat it, but you can bet I won't go trick or treating at his house this year."

Mary laughed.

"We'll talk about it soon Roger, but this isn't over. Good night," she said and hung up.

Mary changed her mind and was waiting at the bus stop the next morning.

"You're like me," Bella said as Mary sat down. "You just can't get enough education."

"I got a phone call last night from a new friend of yours," Mary said.

"Anybody I know?" Bella offered timidly.

"You know very well who I'm talking about," Mary shot back.

"Oh him," Bella said as if her brain finally checked in.

"Tell me exactly what happened and what he said."

In Bella's way of wandering around reality, she slowly related the events of the previous evening, and by the time they arrived at school Mary was formulating a plan. As they approached the school, Mr. Sherman was standing on the steps greeting the incoming students obviously trying to gauge the mood of the student body.

"Good morning ladies, I hope you're feeling better today Mary."

"I apologize for my emotional outburst in your office yesterday Mr. Sherman. Some things have happened since the end of the school day which we need to talk about."

"I'd like that," he said, hoping to get ahead of the next runaway train.

"How about if we have lunch together in the cafeteria, and maybe you could invite Roger Burns to join us. It might help calm down all the people who are looking at us right now," Mary said.

Mr. Sherman looked up and noticed all of the entering students had stopped and were staring at them.

"I'll try and get a hold of Mr. Burns and see if he would care to join us for lunch" he said.

"I think 11:30 would be perfect," said Mary as she and Bella walked up the steps into the building. Once again the rumor mill was churning out every conceivable possibility for the show down in the lunch room.

Four hours later the cafeteria was packed with students, but no one was eating. Mary, Bella, and Mara were sitting in the same place as the day before when Mr. Sherman, followed by Roger approached their table. You could have heard a pin drop as Mr. Sherman reached across the table, shook hands with the three girls and sat down. Roger continued standing. As he looked around the cafeteria and then back at Bella and Mary he said,

"I would like to publicly apologize to Bella Delveccio for demeaning and embarrassing her in front of all of you. It was cruel, and Bella I'm sorry and will never do it again, to anyone."

Bella started crying.

"And to her good and loyal friend Mary Vander Meer,

who by the way is a new student here," Roger started to choke up, "I'm also sorry for trying to embarrass you in front of your new school mates."

Everyone in the cafeteria sat quietly averting eye contact with each other. Some wanted to jump up and shout; others wished they were somewhere else. Mary patted Bella's hand, looked over and winked at Mara.

Roger sat down next to Mr. Sherman feeling more humiliated than he had ever felt in his life. No one in the room moved, feeling as if they had just experienced something very spiritual and cleansing.

"I don't know about the rest of you, but I'm hungry," Mr. Sherman said in a voice loud enough to snap everybody in the room out of their mood.

He was the first one in the food line followed by a unified student body.

The other four of Roger's friends all wrote personal letters to Mary's and Bella's families apologizing for their bad behavior and promising to try and be more considerate to everyone.

Two weeks later, the senior class president transferred to another school district, and in a landslide Mary was elected to the position. With good grades and strong leadership skills she was awarded a full ride scholarship in nursing to Aquinas College for the fall season.

CHAPTER 4

Keith was sitting on the same bench two days later with water dripping off the edge of his umbrella on to the knees of his best jeans.

"There must be something important happening for you to be sitting out in the rain all by yourself," Mary said sliding up next to him and allowing the water from her umbrella to land onto his before traveling to his knees.

"Well, as a matter of fact, this just happens to be one of my favorite haunts, and occasionally I find someone interesting to talk with," he said with kind of a sappy look on his face.

"I don't suppose you would consider continuing this conversation at the coffee shop over on Wealthy Street."

"Is it inside?" Keith asked hopefully.

"I think we can arrange that," She pertly replied.

"My car's parked across the lot," Keith said. "Let's make a run for it."

As they sat at a window table watching the water soaked leaves cover the sidewalk in front of Barney's Coffee and Chat Emporium, Keith couldn't remember when he had been more intrigued. Mary's beautiful blond hair had been soaked by the rain and was stuck to her forehead, but he thought it was perfect. Barney came over and refilled their coffee cups, but they didn't notice.

"Do you want to go for a ride?" Keith asked.

"Where to?" She countered.

"Have you ever seen the west side of Grand Rapids on a rainy day?"

"Am I dressed for it?"

"I'll try and sneak you in," he joked. "With your blond hair you could possibly pass for Polish."

"I'll do my best," she responded.

Keith was proud of his side of town with the sturdy multi-storied houses built decades before. The narrow streets lined with massive old oak and elm trees gave the Polish American stronghold a sense of permanency.

"Two blocks up on the left is the Koski Castle. Let's see if you can guess which one it is," he said.

As he slowed down the rain intensified and the windshield wipers made it difficult for Mary to pick one.

"They all look the same in this deluge, why don't you let me guess from inside your house?"

"Somehow that doesn't seem fair," Keith said.

"Kind of a stickler for rules aren't we?" Mary asked in mock seriousness.

As they walked from the back door through the kitchen shaking off the rain, Mary asked, "What's that smell?"

"That smell, my dear, is the glue that binds this Polish neighborhood together. Its sauerkraut and not the kind you by in cans in the grocery store. Busha makes her own in our basement."

"What's a Busha?"

"She's my grandma, Sophie Koski."

"Is making sauerkraut legal?" Mary asked as if brining cabbage was like making moonshine.

"If it isn't, half of the neighborhood should be in jail," Keith said with a grin on his face. "Would you like to try some?" He asked.

"What's it tasted like?" Mary waffled still not sure if it was safe to eat.

Keith led her down the basement stairs, and showed her the brining crock and the freshly canned quart jars of the European delicacy.

"Come on back upstairs and we'll give it a try."

Keith went to the cupboard; got two bowls, and opened up the oven door. As he slid out the big pan of sauerkraut and roasted pork shoulder, the aroma made her mouth water. Filling the bowls with the steaming delicacy, he set them on the table while Mary grabbed the spoons.

"Is it ready?" Asked Keith's grandma shuffling into the kitchen with a broad smile. "And who is this?" She continued smiling at Mary.

"Busha this is Mary, a friend from college, and Mary," he said with great respect, "this is Busha."

Busha came over and gave the younger woman a warm grandmotherly hug.

"I hope you don't mind that we're eating your dinner," said Mary.

"Keith says I make enough to feed the whole neighborhood, but it never goes to waste," the old woman mused, "and," she pointed a finger at Keith, "You never see anybody with a cold or the flu around here. Am I right?" she said raising her eye brows.

"You're always right, Busha. That's why we all love you," responded Keith as she snickered and ambled back into the living room.

❧

The following Saturday Keith drove across the bridge in downtown Rockford to meet Mary's family. Last fall Keith had played a regional football game at Rockford High School so he was familiar with the area, but had no idea how beautiful Peppler Park was spanning both sides of the Rogue River in the city center. The whole scene was a picture post card with all of the deciduous trees showing off their resplendent colors. As Keith pulled into the driveway, Mary and her dad, who had been sitting on the front steps, stood and walked towards Keith's car.

"Good morning," said Dick Vander Meer, reaching for Keith's hand.

"Good morning to you sir," responded Keith with a firm handshake.

Mary decided that the two men in her life looked good together walking towards the house.

"You may not recognize me, but I'm very familiar with you," said Dick as Mary's mom Betty served them all coffee and cookies on the back deck.

"How so?" asked Keith.

"I told my next door neighbor about you, and he asked if you were the same Keith Koski that tore apart our local football team last fall."

"Well I don't know about tearing anybody up, but I remember we had a pretty good afternoon."

"The way a couple of the boys from church tell it, you were doing most of the tearing."

"They probably didn't remember that the following we got our hats handed to us." Changing the subject Keith said, "You've got a beautiful home here, Mrs. Vander Meer."

"Thank you Keith," she responded. "We've only been in it for a couple of years, but we're really happy to be in

Rockford. It's nice that Mary can commute back and forth to school."

"Are you playing any sports at Aquinas this year?" Dick asked still pleased that he had a local celebrity in his midst.

"No. I wish I had the time," Keith said, "but school's a full time job for me."

"Admirable," said Betty. "What are you majoring in?" She asked.

"Well the file says Business and General Studies, but so far I'm kind of clueless."

"I remember that feeling myself," Dick said.

The conversation waned and Mary took Keith's hand, slid off the couch and said, "We're going to hike the trails by the river while it's still warm."

The foursome all rose, and walked out to Keith's car.

"If you're interested," Betty said, "I cook a mean roasted chicken for Sunday dinner."

Dick smiled and said, "We'd enjoy the company, and the Detroit Lions and Chicago Bears are on T.V."

"If Mary doesn't mind…"

"It's a date," Mary chimed in and they left her folks in the driveway for the day's adventure.

From a fond curiosity to a loving dependency the relationship between Keith and Mary grew. As they studied together to help each other become better in their chosen professions, their love and respect for each other seemed boundless. By their senior years, Mary was spending most of her non-school hours at Keith's home, and she became the daughter Norm and Barbara Koski had always wanted. Sunday dinner was usually at Betty and Dick's and marriage was a subject they all enjoyed talking about. Shortly before Christmas, Mary and Keith began attending Mass at Sacred Heart Church with Keith's folks. Although Mary was raised in the Protestant tradition, they decided together to raise a family as Catholics. After all she thought, it was the same God anyway.

To keep peace in the family and the neighborhood, they made an appointment to talk to Father Mroz.

Father Don, as he was known, was a little surprised that a young couple still wanted to talk to a priest, let alone get married. He offered his benign smile as he ushered them into his office after the last Mass on Sunday.

The young couple took a seat in front of his cluttered desk as the old priest hung his liturgical stole in the closet and joined them.

"So, why do you two kids want to get married?" he asked as he plopped down into his well worn chair pushing away notes from his morning homily to make room for his elbows on the front of his cluttered desk; his chubby hands supporting a visage of kindness and wisdom.

It seemed like sort of a dumb question so the future bride and groom to be kind, lowered their heads and waited for the next question; a real question.

"I can see by the smirks on your faces that you don't think this is a serious subject," he said refusing to move off topic.

"Well," Mary proceeded slowly so as not to get off on the wrong foot, "We love each other," she offered, assuming it was obvious.

"Lots of people love each other," Father countered, "but they all don't run out and tie the knot," he offered raising one eye brow to punctuate the point.

Once again the room was quiet. Keith was pretending to look out the office window, although the stained glass made that impossible.

"We want to have a baby," Mary tried again, hoping

that this approach would allow them to proceed through the priest's gauntlet.

"Have one," the priest said indifferently "Everyone else has, and I don't remember any member of the clergy getting involved or slowing them down."

Father Don slowly pushed himself away from the desk, crossed his leg, and folded his hands across his considerable stomach. "If you just want to legitimize the relationship, go down to City Hall, sign the paper and you can be on your way," he said looking straight at Keith.

The room became smaller as more silence filled the office.

"I'm sorry Father, I'm afraid I just don't know exactly what you're looking for," said the frustrated bride to be.

"Are your parents married?" he asked weaving his fingers behind his head.

They both nodded, hoping there was a light at the end of the tunnel.

Father Don immediately sat up and pulled himself back to the desk.

"Forgive me Mary, and you to Keith," he said, "for being so contrary, but what I am about to tell you is so important that I don't want it to slide over your heads," he paused. "It's no big deal to get hitched. If you are of legal age and sound of mind you can do it anywhere or anytime. But," he emphasized, "and this is the difference," he paused, "the biggest difference. You wonderful young people have decided to marry in God's church and to make Jesus Christ the center of your lives."

"Well…" Mary hedged.

"Think about it!" the priest stressed. "Why do you go to church anyway?"

"Well my folks…"

"Exactly," Father pounced. "Your folks made you because?"

"I don't know, probably because they had to when they were kids," Keith offered lamely.

"Keith, you win the grand prize, but this is what I want you to remember, because it isn't always obvious at your age. They made you come to church because they vowed to make God the center of their lives, and when both of you were born that same blessing was bestowed on you. Understand," he raised his finger again, "when you say 'I do' in the presence of God, you pledge to obey His word and live your lives accordingly. Now, once again, why do you want to get married?"

Keith and Mary began to speak, but were hushed by the priest.

"Don't tell me now," he said lovingly. Go home and talk about it and pray about it, and we'll continue our discussion again next Sunday after Mass."

CHAPTER 5

Johnny Hendricks fidgeted with the waist strap the transporter had placed around him as he slid across the transfer board from his bed to his wheel chair. He was a little put out that the nurses wouldn't let him push himself down to the waiting ambulance, but rules were rules. There was a certain melancholy in Johnny's heart as the young man pushed him down the hall passed the cafeteria. The walls were lined with the crayon drawn pictures from the local grade school kids from the community elementary schools. If it was the children's intent to help pick up the spirits of the patients and their families, they had certainly accomplished their task. Johnny thought that if he ever got his legs working and made it back to Marquette, he would find a way to thank them. His mom, Angie buttoned the collar on his jacket as they blew through the double doors to a rather chilly Marquette morning. It had been a while since Johnnie had felt the fresh air streaming off of Lake Superior, and the contrast of temperatures made him feel a little fragile. There were still patches of snow on the ground, but no one else seemed to notice.

"Time for the next step," Angie said smiling as the transporter pushed Johnny up the ramp into the ambulance to take him to Mary Free Bed Hospital some four hundred miles south in Grand Rapids.

The last six months had been a whirlwind. Last October Johnny had left Grand Rapids and drove up to Hancock, Michigan in the Upper Peninsula with a dream of opening up a youth mission for young people in the area to relax and enjoy each others company. There were two universities as well as several high schools in the area to take advantage of this facility. Johnny's dad and grandpa were both pastors in large churches in the Grand Rapids area, and their congregations had helped fund the mission program. Johnny had managed to find an old building in the historic district of Hancock and after some awkward adjustments between the locals and him, the Mission was created and began to fulfill its purpose. Unfortunately, tragedy struck in February while Johnny was driving a van full of teenagers. They were caught in a snow squall and ran head on into a county snow plow. One teen died, most of the others were injured, and Johnny was flown by MedEvak down to Marquette Hospital with a broken back. Anger and frustration set in and Johnny was unpleasant to be around for a few weeks, but his mom and the hospital staff took it in stride. The anger didn't come so much from his inability to walk as much as from his self imposed guilt. This was the second time in his young life that he had been involved in a fatal car accident and, both times he was the driver. He wasn't angry with God, but he was so sure that his purpose at this stage of his life had been fulfilled by the Hancock Youth Mission that he was just sick inside.

It had seemed so easy these last few months. Everything he did and everyone he met made him feel like Moses leading the Israelites out of Egypt into the Promised Land, but then Moses wasn't allowed to enjoy the land of milk and honey either. Johnny knew he was no Moses, but the Mission seemed like such a great idea to help the youth of the Keweenaw Peninsula. In deed, the mysterious ways in which God was working to fulfill His wonders had Johnny frustrated.

There were snow squalls blowing from the north reminiscent of that terrible day back in February, but Johnny didn't feel any responsibility this time. He was once again falling into his self pity mode without even realizing it. As usual the anger boiled up from within him and the thought of his girl friend Jenny Parvuu with a scar on her head and still wearing a cast on her arm was almost more that he could stand. For the second time in his life he had chosen to block out the death of someone who had trusted him. Young 'Bob the Techie' as all the other members of the Mission leadership called him had never had a chance to grow up. Now he was buried in his hometown of Toronto, Canada with a family and friends to grieve his passing, and Johnny to bear the responsibility. Johnny was raging inside as he held his head down and hoped the ambulance driver looking in the rear view mirror didn't see the tears dripping from his chin on to his new jacket. His mom reached over and handed him a tissue.

The mood soon passed and Johnny considered the one good thing to come from all of this. Like it or not, God had given the Mission to Paul Rader to manage it and Del Souter, the banjo *phenom* to be his right-hand man. The thought of those two fine men working together and enjoying each others company made him smile. He reached out and held his mom's hand as they drove over the Mighty Mac Bridge. It wouldn't be long before he would be with his dad and "Dutch" his Grandpa in Grand Rapids. Between them and his mom they would help figure things out.

☙

It was late in the afternoon when the ambulance exited the expressway onto Wealthy Street in downtown Grand Rapids and immediately came to a stop. It had been quite a while since Johnny had experienced big city grid lock, and he wasn't sure he was ready for the confinement and rigid structuring of a new hospital.

Thirty minutes later the ambulance backed up to another double door and the process of prisoner exchanging began. Dad and Dutch were waiting inside the doors and couldn't wait to get their hands on him.

Dad explained that all of the paper work had been taken care of, and the Grand Rapids version of a transporter pushed him onto an elevator and they all made the trip to the fifth floor. Johnny was impressed by the décor of the hospital and when he was pushed into his single room he was blown away. The room was nicer than many motels he had stayed in and the view towards the Grand River from five stories up was more than he had anticipated. A nurse followed the family into the room and took charge.

"Hi, my names Shelly and I'll be your nurse tonight. If you good folks would like to make yourselves comfortable in the family visiting room down the hall, I'll get Johnny organized and comfortably in bed. I'll come and get you in a few minutes and we'll all have a chance to visit and figure out what we need to know." John and Angie led Dutch down the hall and Shelly turned to Johnny.

"I've heard a lot about you Johnny. You're quite a celebrity," Shelly said helping Johnny slide onto the bed. She took of his shoes and socks and helped him slide off his sweatpants.

After his extended stay in the Marquette Hospital, modesty was a thing of the past. Together they pulled off the Hancock High School Track Team sweatshirt that

Paul Rader and Rod Devlin had given him as a going away present. She helped tie the back of the sleep gown and showed him the drawers where his regular clothes would be kept. She told him to get comfortable and went to fetch his family.

On their way back to Johnny's room, Shelly shook hands with all of them and by the time they entered Johnny's room, they all seemed like old friends.

The three Hendricks' all sat on the plush couch as Shelly explained everything.

"I told Johnny that he was a celebrity around here, but I didn't tell him why," she said. "Actually it has more to do with Dutch. You see, my sister Julie and her husband Dick are members of your church," she said looking at Dutch. "And when you and your son decided to help Johnny create a mission in the U.P., my sister told me and my husband Kenny and we decided to help. So, a few bucks and one unsightly used couch later," she paused and smiled. "We're on your team too. How about that?"

They all looked at Johnny with a dumbfounded look on his face.

"I don't know what to say Shelly," his words stumbled out of his mouth.

"The only thing we all need to say is get to work. A lot of people need you up there," she chided.

"Amen," chortled Dutch hugging his daughter-in-law.

"Praise God," she echoed.

"Praise God indeed," her husband added and they all laughed together.

Just then, a man with a hair net pulled a cart full of food trays in front of Johnny's door, and carried one towards the bed.

"I took the liberty of ordering your dinner an hour ago,"

John said. "I hope you still like chicken fingers and mashed potatoes."

"And eat all of your green beans," Angie added. "You're going to need all the energy you can muster."

As the family rose from the couch, Dad said it was time that they left and let Johnny relax. He invited Shelly to join them in a family prayer.

> *"Father God, we are grateful to You for bringing our son home for some much needed physical help.*
>
> *We know you are the Great Physician and all of our lives are in your hands. We are thankful that you have chosen Shelly, a sister in Christ, to watch over our boy. Make him strong Father so that he can complete the job You asked him to do. Amen."*

Hugs, kisses and goodbyes were shared as the family left Johnny's room.

"I'll let you eat your dinner before it gets cold," Shelly said. "If you need anything I will be right across the hall at my station. Just push the little red button and I will respond over the intercom."

As she left, Johnny opened his chocolate milk and grinned.

Maybe this isn't so bad after all, he thought.

꩜

Johnny woke from a sound sleep dripping with sweat with his night gown twisted uncomfortably around his body. He had no idea what time it was and his room was dark except for the dimmed overhead lights from the hallway. He could hear distant hospital noises and the sound of rubber wheels being pushed along the linoleum covered floor into a room down the hall. A shadow filled the doorway and what appeared to be an older man pushing a dusting broom entered his room and gave the area around Johnny's bed the once over.

Johnny said, "Good Morning, or at least I think its morning."

"I'm sorry I didn't mean to wake you sir," said the voice from the shadows.

"I'm Johnny Hendricks. I just came down from the U.P. to get my legs working again. Doctors up in Marquette said that this was the place to come so they threw me in the back of an ambulance yesterday and here I am."

"Dats a long ride dis time of year," the shadow said. "Anyway I'm sorry I boddered you. I know you need your rest."

"I didn't catch your name," Johnny said as the as the man pushed the dust broom out the door.

"Vic," he said, "Just Vic."

☙

For anyone who has ever spent time as a patient in a hospital, the arrival of the day shift is always painful. The noises of the nighttime hours and the rude awakening of the cheery day shift workers remind you of why you're there and how many times someone had poked or prodded you in the last few hours.

Johnny woke up with this terrible taste in his mouth and the feeling that what ever came next wouldn't be good. He needed a urinal; he needed to sit up; most of all he needed to talk to someone he could confide in. Foot traffic was heavy outside his room, but nobody seemed interested in him.

There must be somebody who is assigned to me to take care of my needs, or at least let me know that I'm on somebody's schedule, he anguished.

Johnny pulled the blanket over his head to shut out the world and wept.

Why had all of this happened to me, He sobbed. *Things were going so well. I had everything under control. So many people were counting on me and now…*

"Hello is any body in there," a warm friendly female voice asked from the other side of the blanket.

"I'm not receiving visitors this morning," he offered lamely.

"Will then how will the chef know how to cook your eggs?" came the response, or whether you want real sausage or turkey sausage. These are important decisions. Can you help me out?"

"Give me a minute, will you?" came a muffled voice from under the sheet.

"I'll tell you what. I've got to go next door and deliver some ice water. I'll be right back and we'll start over again, okay?"

With that she was gone and Johnny knew he didn't have much time to pull himself together.

God, You sure know how to make a big shot feel like a little shot, he thought racing to make himself presentable to this unknown care giver with a nice voice.

"Excuse me," said the voice a few moments later, "my names Claire. Would you happen to be Johnny Hendricks from Marquette?"

"Claire, I'm very sorry for behaving so poorly but I'm a

little overwhelmed by all of this. I'm afraid I'm not dealing very well with my lack of mobility."

And then he began to sob again.

"I'm sorry too," she said sitting on the edge of the bed, "but how are you supposed to feel. You've been through a horrible tragedy. You're lucky to be alive. Your body is full of some serious drugs; you're exhausted and you're alone. I personally don't see too much to smile about, do you?"

She handed him a Kleenex and Johnny blew his nose.

"'First of all I'm going to change your urinal and elevate your bed, then I'm going to get rid of the night shirt that's strangling you and find you some shorts and a T-shirt, okay."

"I'm such a baby," Johnny said accepting another Kleenex.

"You'd better give yourself a pat on the back. After all you've been through you might very well be one of the toughest guys I've ever met."

Johnny smiled and shook his head. A few minutes later he slid his transfer board from his bed to his wheel chair and pushed himself into his own personal bathroom to brush his teeth and clean up.

"I took the liberty of ordering your breakfast," said Claire through the door.

"What did I end up with," he shouted through the door.

"What?"

"What kind of sausage did you order?"

"Pork sausage; you're not sick enough to get the turkey sausage," she said jokingly.

"Thanks," he said pushing himself back into the room.

"Your schedule is on your T.V. screen," she said pointing to the box on the wall. "After breakfast someone will wheel you down to Dr. Van Every's office. She's your neurologist and has all of your x-rays and paper work from Marquette.

I'm sure after she welcomes you she'll give you the guided tour of the facilities and introduce you to some of the people you'll be working with. I think you're going to be impressed. Oh," she said looking at the doorway. Here's your breakfast now. Would you like to stay in your chair, or would you prefer to sit up in bed?"

The transporter knocked on the door and pushed Johnny up to Dr. Van Every's desk, and returned to the hallway.

"Good Morning Johnny," said a pretty thirty something African American dressed in scrubs and a lab coat with her hand outstretched. Johnny could tell when she stood to come around the desk that she was either a tri-athlete or marathoner or something like that, and when she gripped his hand he was impressed.

"Your reputation precedes you sir. You are the talk of the hospital."

Once again Johnny couldn't figure out what all the fanfare was about.

"People keep talking about my reputation; I feel like I'm in the witness protection program. Can you tell me what's so important about this gimp in a wheel chair?"

Well, between all the mail you've received and the number of phone calls from all over the state, it seems to me that you must be a PIP."

"What's a PIP?" Johnny asked.

"A pretty important person," the doctor said with a smile. "Now let's take a tour of our fabulous facility and introduce you to a few specialists who are going to put you back on your feet."

As Dr. Van Every pushed him down the hallway, an older

woman in a South High School tee shirt and sweatpants balancing under an overhead rail slowly approached.

"Hi Doc," she said doing her best to keep from falling while trying to stay vertical as her trainer did his best to keep her moving forward. By the grimace on her face, it was obvious that her pain was almost more than she could tolerate.

"Good Morning Mimi," greeted Dr. Van Every. "How are we doing?"

"Never better," the woman replied sucking up the pain with a little false bravado.

"Keep on pushing," the neurologist said, "you're almost out of here."

The trainer nodded to the doctor as they passed.

"Will I be doing that?" Johnny asked.

"If I told you that it might help you to walk again, would you give it a try?" She asked as she pushed him into one of the physical therapy rooms.

Without responding, he was immediately taken aback by the size of the room and the number of therapists working with patients. The facility was organized into different stations; each one designated for a different physical function. Johnny watched a man Grandpa Dutch's age sitting on a huge red ball trying to maintain his balance. Another station had a little boy trying to pick up a deck of cards, one at a time. Everyone smiled and nodded at Johnny as he tried his best to accept this new phase of his life.

"Seen enough?" the doctor asked pushing him through an exit door on the other side of the room.

"When can I get started?" He asked enthusiastically.

"I think I saw on your schedule that you would work with Mary right after lunch. She was the therapist working with the older gentleman on the balance ball."

"She looked familiar," he said as they made their way back to her office to look at his x-rays.

Johnny's mom Angie was sitting on the couch in his room glancing at a day old copy of the Grand Rapids Press when the transporter helped him back into bed.

"Good Morning mom," Johnny said without much enthusiasm.

"Rough night?" Angie asked, walking over to the bed to help her son under the sheets.

Johnny nodded.

"You look a little down," she said. "Is everything all right?"

"I just keep thinking of where I'm supposed to be," he said looking away from her.

"Do you know something I don't know?"

"I've just got so much to do," he said emphatically. "Don't you understand?"

"You know I could give you a pep talk or offer you some Christian platitudes from the Book of Proverbs, but I don't think that would raise your spirits," she said taking his hand. "It goes without saying that you're depressed and wish you had a little more control over your body and your life, but in the twenty five years that you've been on this planet, when has that ever happened. When I hear you say "I", I'm not sure your heart's in the right place. This odyssey you've been living for the last six months has been about you following Christ, not you being his mission foreman. Ah, here comes your lunch."

Perfect timing, he thought as the server placed his lunch on the tray next to the bed. Johnny was so used to having all the answers and everything going his way that he had forgotten that life was in God's time, and His will be done.

Angie quietly turned around and returned to the couch.

Bowing his head he prayed,

> *"Father God, I can't imagine there is anyone dumber or more self centered than I am. I humbly apologize to you and to my mom for forgetting who I am, and Whose I am. Please help keep me focused on your Word, as well as your work so that I might better serve You. Bless the good people who prepared this lunch so that I can regain my health to help do your good deeds. Amen"*

"Now that sounds like the Johnny I know," said Angie, as a young woman entered the room.

CHAPTER 6

"**G**ood Heavens," said Mary Vander Meer staring at Johnny and putting her hand over her mouth.

Johnny looked up at the young woman with a clip board and didn't immediately make the connection. When she took her hand away from her mouth it all came rushing back to her; the joy, the panic, the blackness, the sorrow, the emptiness, the guilt.

"Mary," he whispered under his breath as a million thoughts raced through his brain with none of them making any sense.

Angie didn't recognize Mary. She had only met her once and it had been so long ago.

Mary slowly walked to the bed with tears streaming down her face.

"I'm so sorry," she said. "I couldn't stay... Bill...Amy," she sobbed with her hands over her mouth.

Johnny hushed the sobs embracing Mary as tenderly as he could. "Mary, Mary, Mary, you have nothing to be sorry for. It wasn't anybody's fault."

"Oh," she jumped back in embarrassment, "I'm going to

hurt you," she said, taking a napkin from his tray and drying her eyes.

"I'm sorry for acting like such a baby, please don't tell my boss, she'll have a fit," Mary said turning to Angie. "I'm sorry," she said addressing Angie, "We met once before, along time ago."

Angie stood and hugged Mary. "I remember. That was a much happier time. How are you Mary?"

"Well, I was fine until now, I'm sorry, I kind of had that all buried in the past and it sort of knocked me down," she said apologetically. "Let me go splash a little water on my face and pull myself together and I'll come back and the three of us can go down to the therapy gym and start making a walker out of a sitter, okay?"

Looking at the face in the bathroom mirror frightened Mary. Her hands were still trembling. She tried desperately to separate the cob webs of the past and struggled to gain enough control to go back into Johnny's room and do her job. There really wasn't a great deal to remember about the relationship between her, Bill, Johnny and Amy. Love and friendships seemed to be a part of their daily lives back then, and suddenly that world was shattered. She couldn't bring back those thoughts and memories. She really couldn't.

Mary walked back into Johnny's room and Angie was gone.

"Where'd your mom go?" Mary asked.

"She said we had some things to talk about, and you could collect her in the visitor's room when we were ready to start the therapy."

"I don't know what to say," Mary said awkwardly looking out the window at the Grand Rapids skyline.

"Where did you go?" Johnny asked trying to quell the anxiety that was slowly filling the room.

Mary turned, took his hand, and slowly began recounting the tale of despair, fear and uncertainty after the accident and the decision by her family to move to Rockford and begin a new life. She told him of her attempts to contact him, but never having the courage to complete the calls. Once again, there seemed like nothing to say. Johnny pulled her towards him and together they sobbed through their inability to stop the floodgates of despair. This pain was bigger than either of them could handle. They held each other and yet both felt very much alone. They had both built this barricade of anguish for themselves and weren't sure they wanted to tear it down. Johnny was speechless as the memories of the accident began flooding into his vulnerable state of mind. The glib youth leader with all of the answers was suddenly lost in a vacuum of self pity and anger, and there was nothing he could say or do to erase these terrible feelings. Mary handed Johnny a Kleenex and together they both blew their noses and began to laugh.

"What's so funny?" Mary asked sniffling behind a wad of tissue.

"I don't know," Johnny said.

"Me either," she responded squeezing his hand.

"We'd better throw some water on our faces and go collect mom. She's probably wondering what's going on," he said in a husky voice.

The two emotionally exhausted old friends who had opened up a nightmare headed for the visitors room.

☙

The Mary Free Bed Home had begun as a simple idea back in 1891. A small group of socially conscious women in the city of Grand Rapids got together and passed a purse around to anyone named Mary, or anyone who knew someone named Mary, to donate a dime to help people of limited means to attain hospital care. Since Mary was the most popular female name at the time, they soon had enough money for the first Mary Free Bed in a local hospital. By 1911, more women had joined and together created the Mary Free Bed Guild. As the organization grew, they became a children's orthopedic center, and in the ensuing decades added services for amputees and finally adult treatments for spinal chord injuries and stroke victims. The modern six story non-profit rehab center now has 167 beds as well as out patient facilities.

Mary pushed Johnny into the visitor's room where Angie was sitting alone with her head bowed in prayer. The two waited until Angie finished.

"I'm so sorry to add to your shock," Angie said, "but seeing you together have brought back a lot of terrible memories which I admit I'm not dealing very well with either. I think it's important to offer this up to God and ask for help and comfort." Angie offered her hands to Mary and Johnny.

> *"Father God, we come to you with feelings and emotions that we don't understand and are having trouble dealing with. You truly are the Great Physician, and know all things so we ask for your guidance. Calm our hearts and ease the pain we are all feeling. Help us to take this opportunity to heal our wounds and move forward to embrace this new relationship with Mary. We thank you for putting yourself in all of our lives to help bring glory to You. All that we are, and all that we have we offer up to You, Father. Amen"*

"Thank you, that was beautiful," Mary said squeezing Angie's hand.

"Let's see if we can go and get this young fellow to break a sweat," Angie said holding open the visitor's room door.

∽

Johnny was emotionally drained, and it wasn't long before his body was taxed as well. Although the therapists at Marquette General had kept his upper body limber, the two months of riding the wheel chair had taken its toll. The new regimen of core exercises and lower leg therapy was almost more than he could handle, but Mary knew his limitations and with expertise and lots of encouragement helped him to endure. So many times in the first few weeks he was ready to quit, and accept his future as an invalid, but being surrounded by patients of all ages who were worse off than he was, not to mention the daily help from mom and dad, helped bolster his spirits. A week later with sweat dripping off his nose from doing core exercises, Johnny's mom and girl friend Jenny walked into the gym.

"You're not going to get any better by laying on your backside and smoozing the ladies," Jenny said planting a kiss on his damp forehead.

"It's wonderful to see you Jenny; when did you get in?" Johnny asked.

"Your mom and dad picked me up at the bus station at 11:30 last night," she said. "How are you feeling?" She asked caressing his cheek.

"Oh," he said as an after thought. "This is Mary, my physical therapist.

Mary reached out and shook Jenny's hand.

"Angie has told me what a wonderful therapist and friend you are," Jenny said.

"Friend," Johnny said. "Are you kidding? She spends every day trying to kill me. Do you see this sweat on my face? She did that."

"Still a whiner I see," Jenny said with a smirk on her face.

"Mom, it's impossible to get any sympathy from any of the women in my life," he said in mock exasperation.

"Poor baby," Angie murmured.

"Actually, we came to help with the therapy. What can we do?" Angie asked Mary.

"Well bless your hearts," Mary said. "Angie if you want to show Jenny how to do the leg lifts; I'll go over and finish some paper work."

Looking at the young lovers Angie said, "I think I'll go make a phone call while you two catch up."

"I love you," Jenny said sitting down next to Johnny.

"I love you too," Johnny said nuzzling Jenny's neck. "I was afraid you'd forget about me."

"Fat chance of that," she said, with Helen coming over every day to ask if I've heard anything from you."

"I know an apology doesn't mean much, but I just can't get it together," Johnny said with his head down. "I'm just furious all the time. As hard as I try, it just feels like everything is slipping away. I know everybody's pulling for me, it's just... oh I don't know."

Jenny rubbed his shoulders. "Is it Mary?" That had to be a big shock having the memory of that horrible night dragged up again."

"I'm sure that's part of it, but then there's Bob. I killed him too. I think God is punishing me," he sniffled, "and He's doing a pretty good job, don't you think?"

"I think we need to talk to somebody about all of this.

I'm not saying that it all didn't happen; I just don't think that you're responsible. I think we should talk to your dad and see if he has any ideas."

"I'm sorry Jenny, I just can't…"

"Why don't you try lifting your leg with this hoist? That's something we can do together."

❧

"The following night John Hendricks called Ernie Sugg up in Houghton. His wife Brenda answered the phone.

"Is this the chief cook and bottle washer at the Sugg house?"

"Dat and a whole lot more," she chuckled. "Who is dis?"

"This is Johnny Hendricks' dad down in Grand Rapids. How are you Brenda?"

"Oh don't tell me there's something wrong with Johnny."

"Well, it concerns Johnny. I wonder if Ernie's home this evening?" John asked.

"Ernie," she hollered into the other room, "telephone for you. It's Johnny Hendricks' dad."

"Hello John," Ernie said picking up the phone. "I hope everything's all right."

"Hello Ernie, we've got kind of a situation down here and you were the first one I thought of. If memory serves me right, you lost part of your leg fighting in Iraq, is that right?"

"Yah, it seems like a long time ago. They shipped me to Walter Reed Hospital for a new one," he joked. "Wait a minute, their not cutting off Johnny's legs are they?"

"No, nothing quite as drastic as that I'm happy to say. His legs will be fine. In fact they are making excellent progress with his mobility. I'm afraid his biggest problem is between his ears."

"John I think I know what you're gonna say," Ernie said.

"Ernie, I know you'll keep this between you and Brenda, but Johnny feels responsible for the death of Bob, the Canadian boy who died in the crash. I don't know if you heard, but when Johnny was a junior in high school, he was driving on a double date, and swerved to avoid a deer. The car slid off the road and his girl friend and best buddy were killed. Now it's happened again. Do you see where I'm going with this? Lying in a bed at Walter Reed with a bunch of busted up soldiers there must have been some PTSD around the wards. Did it happen to you or any of your buddies?"

"You know John that was a long time ago. I know we had classes and counseling," Ernie paused. "To tell you the truth, I didn't want to come home, and many of them were much worse off than me. I wasn't ashamed of what I did, but I didn't look forward to a pity party either. I mean I was the toughest defenseman on the Tech hockey team. I wasn't gonna have anybody carry my bag, you know what I mean?"

There was silence on both ends of the line.

"You know Johnny's a special kid. I mean he's so gentle with people, but he knows when to stand up. You know what I'm saying."

"Yes Ernie, I know exactly what you're saying. What you've just shared with me means an awful lot. Angie and I can take it from here. I really appreciate your friendship and confidence. God bless you Ernie and thank you. Good night."

"What did he say?" Angie asked.

"He said our boy needs help," John said quietly. "I'll call the doctor in the morning."

☾

"Vic is that you?"

Without a sound Vic's big body blocked the light in the hallway.

"Sorry Johnny, I didn't mean to wake you."

"You didn't wake me. I was waiting for you to come by."

"Why's dat?" Vic asked dusting under the couch by the window.

"Cause you talk funny. You talk like a Yooper."

"Well I been dare," he stopped and leaned on his broom, "a long time ago."

"What part of the U.P.?"

"Oh, here and dare."

"Have you been to the Keweenaw Peninsula?"

Vic made a swipe under the bed and quickly left the room.

The next morning after breakfast Jenny entered Johnny's room, pushed the wheel chair up to the bed and said "up and at em big boy we're burnin daylight."

"This must be a dream. I'm having a vision of an angel in my room," he said sweetly.

"Save that stuff for the hired help. We've got work to do."

"I love you Jenny."

"I love you too, now move!"

As the two lovers blew through the gym door, Mary was waiting by the huge cushioned pad unrolling a long strip of wide rubber band.

"Are you ready to loosen up those muscles?" Mary asked.

"Me or her," he said pointing over his shoulder.

"I think we'll start with you, okay?"

With a grimace on his face, Johnny did everything he

could to elevate his lower body, but this morning wasn't a good one.

"Maybe we should take a little break and tell Mary about the Mission," Johnny pleaded.

Mary nodded knowing it was time to ease up.

"Well," Jenny said as the three of them sat down on the big mat,

"Summer has finally arrived in the Keweenaw, and the black flies are biting everything in sight. The Upper Peninsula State Bird, the (Mosquito) is just beginning to raise his ugly head, and the smelt are running up the streams from Lake Superior. Nobody is jumping into the lakes yet, but we have stopped wearing our snow shoes and parkas."

"What's a smelt?" Mary asked.

"It's a tasty little fish that swims up the streams after spending all winter in Lake Superior. You can only net them early in the summer."

"Do you mind if we talk about the Mission?" Johnny asked.

"You wouldn't believe it," Jenny said. "Paul and Del have got the place open from 9 A.M. to 9 P.M. with the game area actually crowded in the evening. There are as many girls as there are boys. The Houghton Youth Mission has become the "in" place to be. In fact, Bob Heikinen, the council president said we may have to create some new parking lots. What do you think about that?"

"I'm really impressed. I had no idea your Mission was that important," Mary said.

"God has really blessed us with such powerful new leadership," Johnny said.

"You know, I think you might have had a little something to do with that too," Jenny added.

"It's becoming obvious that Paul and Del can run that place better than I ever could," he said.

Mary looked at Jenny.

"Are we invited to the party?" Jenny asked.

"What party is that?" Johnny shot back.

"The pity party Johnny Hendricks is having with himself right now," Jenny said looking away.

The moment was ruined and Jenny headed for the exit.

"Let's get you back in your chair and you can catch her at the elevator," Mary said.

"I don't know why," Johnny groused, "all we do is fight anymore."

"That wasn't a fight Johnny. That was a woman who loves you and can't figure out why you want to give up."

Johnny pushed himself into the hallway and Jenny was leaning against a wall talking on the phone.

"Who are you talking to?" He asked pulling up along side of her.

"I'm trying to get a hold of your mom. She dropped me off thinking I'd be here most of the day."

"Would you please come back to the gym? I'm sorry, I just can't figure out what's going on in my stupid head."

"Johnny you need help. We both need help to get you back to where you belong. And I'm not talking about just physical help. I love you and I'm not going anywhere, but you've got some demons in that wonderful head of yours and we've got to get them out."

"Please don't leave me Honey. You're all I've got and all I want," he said squeezing her hand.

Jenny bent down and kissed him tenderly, and said, "C'mon we're heading back to the salt mines."

Later in the day John, Angie, and Dutch walked into his room while he was taking a nap, and Jenny was watching T.V.

"Is he asleep?" Angie asked.

"Yeah it's been a rough day so far," Jenny said quietly.

"We've talked to the doctors and made an appointment for all of us to speak with a psychologist this afternoon," said John.

"I'm not sure I should go with you," Jenny said. "After all I'm not really a member of the family," she said.

"You two mean more to each other than most married couples I know," said Dutch with a grandfatherly smile.

"Who's a married couple?" Johnny asked waking from a sound sleep.

"Certainly not you and me, Buster," Jenny chortled. "You're too bad, and I'm too good," she said playfully.

"That's telling him sister," said Angie.

"I feel like I missed part of the conversation," said Johnny scratching his head with a befuddled look on his face.

CHAPTER 7

Dr. Van Every walked into Johnny's room a half hour later and together they all went down to the conference room to discuss Johnny's brain. Dr. Van Every introduced Dr. Phillips to the Hendricks family and Jenny, and then left the room.

"I understand you've had kind of a rough go," the Doctor said speaking to Johnny.

There was a silence you could cut with a knife.

"I'm not sure where to start or what to say," Johnny began looking at his hands. "I'm not the old fun loving Johnny that I used to be, and I'm either furious or weeping like a baby most of the time," he grumbled.

"Any thoughts on why you're angry? Were you angry before you arrived here?" The doctor asked.

"I'm sure it started with the accident," Johnny said as if that was obvious to everyone but the doctor himself.

"Tell me about the accident."

"Not much to tell," said Johnny. "I killed a friend of mine."

"Did you kill him, or did he die as a victim in a car wreck?"

"What difference does it make? I was responsible. I

mean if I hadn't been driving we wouldn't be here right now. Would we?" Johnny lashed out.

"Did you kill him on purpose?" Dr. Phillips aggressively volleyed back, folding his arms across his chest.

Jenny began weeping for the loss of the young Canadian boy she hardly knew. She tried to take Johnny's hand but he pushed her away.

Johnny wanted to accept full responsibility for the tragedy, but something in the back of his head kept telling him that God had let him down. He just sat there in silence waiting for everyone in the room to pass judgment on him. He knew he deserved it.

"You think it's easy to live with" he ranted belligerently, "but this happened before, and now I've got someone else to remind me of that terrible night." Johnny said alluding to Mary as he sunk deeper into his sour mood as the tears began to flow.

"I think I've heard enough to establish that we are dealing with a form of PTSD," the doctor said. "Most people think that Post Traumatic Stress is a wartime condition which only happens to combat soldiers, but automobile accidents are an even more prevalent cause."

"Is it treatable?" Angie asked commiserating with her son across the table.

"Yes, and with a very high success rate," Doctor Phillips said trying to comfort the family. "I've got a film I want you all to watch to help you understand what we're all dealing with. I'm going to prescribe some medication to help ease some of the anxiety, and tomorrow morning you and I will begin tackling the problem," he said looking at Johnny. The Doctor stood, started the film and as he passed Johnny, gave his shoulder a gentle squeeze as he left the room.

Dr. Van Every stuck her head into the conference room

after the film. "I've ordered hot fudge sundaes for all of us in the cafeteria. Therapy has officially been canceled for the rest of the day," she said with a smile.

Later in the afternoon, Mary came into Johnny's room with a fresh ice water.

"Do you need a nap?" She asked.

"No it's been kind of good and crazy at the same time today."

"Hey, I've got someone I want you to meet. He said he'd be down in a minute."

"And who is my new visitor?"

"The love of my life and the father of my daughter Amy," Mary smiled.

"That sounds like my cue to come in," said a new face in a business suit. "Hi, I'm Keith Koski, and I take full responsibility for this woman you've been dealing with."

Johnny and Keith shook hands and Keith joined Mary on the couch.

"It's nice to finally meet you in person. You're all my wife has talked about for the last few weeks."

"It must have been a pretty dull conversation," Johnny said.

"Not really, you seem to have done some extraordinary things in the Upper Peninsula lately, and now I'm told we're going to drive some 600 miles up to the Keweenaw Peninsula after you return just to eat pasties and swat mosquitoes," he said in mock seriousness.

"Your family would be very welcome," Johnny said, "And the pasties are worth the trip."

"Seriously, from everything I've heard, you're doing great work. I'm sorry you got knocked down, but it sounds like you needed a breather. When you get back on your feet we would both like you to come out to Rockford for dinner and a visit? Mary here has turned into a pretty decent Polish cook, haven't you Honey?" He said kissing her on the cheek.

"You'd better get home and start dinner while Johnny and I plan our trip north," she said smugly.

Keith took his cue; got up; shook Johnny's hand, and headed for home.

"Where'd you guys meet?" Johnny asked.

"Just up the road at Aquinas," she said.

"You seem very happy," he said.

"After the accident, life wasn't worth living," she said somberly. "And it's happened to you twice. Anything, I repeat anything I can do to help get you up and running, count on me."

☙

Johnny was reading the Gideon Bible he had found in a drawer by his bed when he heard a tap on his door.

"Yer up awful late," said Vic.

"I was waiting for you."

"Why's dat?" Vic asked.

"Cause you remind me of where I live."

"In da U.P.?"

"In Hancock."

"Ah dat's a nice town."

"Do you know it?"

"A little bit."

"Do you know R.J. Hackala?"

"How'd you know?" Victor asked taken aback.

"The name Victor and the accent, gave it away."

"You gonna turn me in?"

"For what?" Johnny asked. "You didn't kidnap Jimmy so the F.B.I. isn't looking for you. R.J. explained the whole thing to the local police so their not after you. The whole Hackala family's doing fine. I'm sure we could restore your good name and you could come home. How does that sound?"

"You know I miss da people up dare. It's da only place I've ever lived," he said.

"How'd you end up in Grand Rapids sweeping floors?"

Victor Wurtz sat down on the sofa with the broom between his knees and told his life story.

"I was born in L'Anse. My folks were immigrants from Germany back in da 30's," Victor leaned back on the couch, took out a hanky and blew his nose. "Da U.P. was a beautiful place to live back den. Everybody was a European immigrant and grateful to live in America. No kings or kaisers or people telling you what to do. Everybody spoke a strange kind of English with words from all of our cultures. Dare were Germans, Finns, Poles, and Welsh, plus da folks who had been dare a long time. Everybody was just trying to get tru da depression. And den da war came. I was just a little kid. I'm sure my folks talked about it, but never in front of me and my brudder Klaus. When da Americans got involved tings started to change. My kid brudder Klaus started getting into fights at school. We didn't know who Hitler was, but dat didn't matter. Den one night people we didn't even know burned down our house and barn and we were on da run. We ran into da night with da fire lighting up da sky behind us. Some folks put us up for da night, and da next morning my dad called a friend and asked him if he would take me. I never saw my folks again," he said blowing his nose again. "The Aittama's, that was dare name," he paused again thinking back, "dey treated me like I was dare own son. Life was okay, but I never forgot my folks and Klaus. I eventually inherited da house and property from dem and created a car parts business, and dat's when I got in trouble with da law.

It wasn't really trouble for me because nobody knew I was selling stolen car parts, except for da victims. When I ran into R.J., he reminded me of myself when I was a teenager. Nobody loved him; nobody cared. I offered him a chance to make a little money and he jumped at da opportunity. He was really good at it," Vic said smiling. "Of course it all came to an end when he got caught stealing a battery and had to drop off his little brudder Jimmy at my place."

"Why didn't you call his mother?" Johnny asked.

"Hah," he said smiling at Johnny.

"She was da problem. R.J. tawt little Jimmy was safer with me den wid her. Well dat sure didn't work out, and long story short, I sold everyting and got out of town. You know da rest."

"How did you end up in Grand Rapids?" Johnny asked.

"Dis is da funny part," said Vic enjoying the story. "I had dis friend in Marquette from da junk business, and his brudder in-law was a cop. So on my way south, I asked him to see if he could find a Klaus Wurtz tru da State Registry, and sure enough up jumps Klaus's name in Kent County. I called his number and his son answer's da phone. I say dis is your Uncle Victor, your dad's brudder. Well, da next ting you know, me and Burt, my dog, are in Grand Rapids visiting my long lost family. Klaus is a widower and living with his son and his family. They say, Sure I can stay in my camper next to da house until I can find someting permanent. I spend Christmas wid my family, and because I've got a few bucks, and dare not doing too good financially, everyting's just fine. Den in February, Klaus's granddaughter Greta gets in a car wreck and ends up in Mary Free Bed. Anyway, we're all visiting her and I notice a sign dat says dare hiring here, so I'm tinkin, she'll be here for a while, and I'm not doing nuttin," he says lifting his hands. "And den da real kicker;

you show up. I hear dis buzz around da hospital cafeteria dat dis preacher from da Upper Peninsula is rehabbing here so I put two and two togedder, and Johnny Hendricks is lyin in a bed two floors above Gretta."

Victor leaned forward, put his hands on his knees and offered Johnny a satisfying smile. "Don't dat beat all?"

"But why a sweeper?" Johnny asked.

"Dey weren't hiring anymore brain surgeons dat day," Victor laughed, "and da money dey were payin didn't interest anybody else. Unemployment and welfare paid more, so dey was grateful to get an old codger like me. I been tinkin 'bout askin for a raise," he joked.

"If these good folks only knew what a bargain you are," Johnny mused.

"Well, I ain't telling em," Victor said in a mock uproar.

"Victor, God bless you for looking me up. Believe it or not, you're a touch of home."

"Johnny I gotta scoot or I'll be losin my job, and dare ain't much for an old Yooper to do down here in civilization. I'll be back tomorrow night and you can tell me about R.J. and Jimmy," and with that he was gone.

☙

From nine until ten every morning Mary worked her magic on Johnny's body and from ten until eleven Dr. Phillips worked on Johnny's PTSD. He preferred the mental sessions over the muscle therapy. The more Mary exhausted his muscles the more it hurt. It was like being friends with the torturer.

They stopped for lunch and a short nap, and the afternoon was much the same as the morning. The evenings were filled with laughter and competition as his folks and

Dutch bounced in with some new board game to challenge their minds. Jenny had taken the bus back to Hancock the day before and Johnny wondered how he could make it without her. It was an experience he had never felt before and couldn't remember what life was like a year ago when he was free to do what ever he wished. He was no longer free. He wanted to be with Jenny.

Dr. Phillips turned out to be kinder than Johnny had originally thought, and was patient while Johnny earnestly tried to uncover the thoughts and feeling he had buried from the past. As the petals of the flower were peeled back, it became clearer that Johnny had become a much different person than before the first accident. Together they found out that Johnny was a more happy-go-lucky and less responsible teenager before the crash, and the sudden deaths of his best friend and girl friend caused him to blame himself because he was the driver. Surely there was something he could have done to avoid the deer. In the clear light of day he was a murderer, and any way you chose to paint it, that was the unvarnished truth. More importantly, the reconciliation between he and his God to absolve him from his assumed guilt lay at the foundation of his core beliefs, and it was becoming evident that he wanted to suffer the pain on his terms and not accept the simple forgiveness that God offered through his Son Jesus. It was as if Johnny was saying to himself, *I'll let you know when you're forgiven, and it won't be for a long time.* Johnny felt like he was peeking out of his closet asking for permission to come into the light. But now he did it again. Before he had a chance to atone for his first sin he had killed another friend; the same way. His brain simply exploded again, and he was more furious than ever. *What did I do to deserve this?* He silently shouted to his loving God. He talked to his dad and his grandpa who were the theologians in the family and together they prayed for an answer to release Johnny from this self denunciation he had placed upon himself, and allow God to open the floodgates of redemption which he needed to fulfill his mission.

CHAPTER 8

The wind was blowing out of the northeast creating choppy whitecaps like a washboard on Marquette Bay. Paul Rader, Johnny's stand-in as the director at the Mission in Hancock, had driven down to Marquette to pick up a few donations from the local church association and pick up Jenny at the bus terminal.

Paul was one of the greatest gifts and friends God had given Johnny to help run the Mission. The sudden death of Paul's young son, and abandonment by his wife had taken all of the joy from his life in Birch Creek down in south eastern Michigan. As a middle school teacher and track coach, a mid-term job opened up in Hancock and a new start was the perfect opportunity to escape the past.

It was a lonely, job driven existence for a single man in the U.P. until an announcement in the local Mining Gazette News Paper led him to Johnny and the Mission. They became friends, and when Johnny was crippled in the car accident, Paul volunteered to temporarily replace him, and took a leave of absence from teaching.

He had called Johnny's dad down in Grand Rapids the night before to give him an up date on the Mission and to find out how Johnny was doing. John explained that Jenny was coming home the next day on the afternoon bus, so Paul volunteered to pick her up in Marquette, and after eight hours on the bus, she was happy to see a familiar face. After loading her baggage in the back of his truck, they headed north for the Keweenaw. An hour later they stopped for dinner in Ishpeming at Buck's Restaurant, a local landmark with antlers on the walls, and Lake Superior white fish on the menu.

"So, I'm all ears," said Paul stabbing a French fry with his fork. "What's your prognosis for our friend in Mary Free Bed?"

Jenny stirred her soda with a red plastic straw, and contemplated what she wanted to say.

"I wish I had the complete answer, but it seems to change from moment to moment. Physically I think he'll be fine. That hospital is the most incredible rehab facility I've ever seen. They have him doing something positive every minute of the day. I don't know if Johnny's dad told you, but his physical therapist is Mary Koski. She was the other survivor in the car-deer wreck that killed Johnny's girl friend and his best buddy back in high school." Jenny paused dipping a piece of fish in tartar sauce and savoring the distinct flavor. "She had a rough time recovering from the accident. She was unhurt physically, but it took a year of counseling before she could face the world. She did manage to get back on track, get her therapy degree, and marry a great guy. The day she walked into his room for the first time and met Johnny, she lost it. Can you imagine the shock they felt seeing each other for the first time seven years after the accident?"

"It's a wonder the shock didn't kill them both," Paul said.

"Actually after they got used to the idea that they were the survivors and were both in a better place, they accepted the blessing for what it was."

Jenny stopped talking as the waitress offered the dessert menu and presented the bill. Both declined, paid the bill and went out into the cool U.P. air. Jenny wished she had worn a heavier coat as she walked to the car. Just another adjustment she thought. Paul turned the heater on as they continued heading north. They were both quiet as the moon shadowed the giant pines along the roadside.

Jenny broke the silence. "You know Paul, when we both met Johnny he was the Master of the Universe. It seemed like he was God's right hand. I'm still amazed at some of the things which happened to him and around him," she paused trying to make sense of what she was thinking. "I mean, I'm just a small town Yooper girl who's never been anywhere, and when Johnny waltzed into the motel where I was working to pick up his stuff that first evening, he swept me off of my feet. And in the days that followed, it was as if God had personally sent another Moses to deliver His people. To say that I was enthralled would be an understatement. Everyone and everything he needed was somehow placed at his feet. I mean the first person he met was Helen Aho, and two hours later he was leasing her building where the Mission now stands. To say that the building was derelict is an understatement. I mean look at it now; it's the Taj Mahal of the Keweenaw Peninsula," Jenny said starring out the window at the all consuming darkness.

"You know, when I walked into that hollowed out shell of a building to offer up my services to help build a mission, I really didn't know that I was the one who needed help, but he did." Paul said. "He really didn't ask any prying questions. He just gave me that old Johnny smile, took all of our hands and offered up a prayer. The next day I had to go back to teaching at the middle school, but I would have given anything to be down in the basement of that Mission building shelves with R.J. and Del. And when he offered to take me home for Christmas, everything in my body told me not to accept, but he made it sound like I was doing him a favor."

Jenny could see Paul smiling through the head lights of an oncoming car.

"You asked me how Johnny was doing," Jenny said breaking the silence. The truth is I don't know," she said with tears in her eyes. "Johnny doesn't have an enemy in the world except for himself. He's like a ticking time bomb. He jumps at any excuse he can find to demean himself, and no amount of help or praise can change his mind. I get so frustrated with him sometimes I could just scream; in fact sometimes I do," she said sheepishly. "He has therapists working on his body and psychiatrists working on his head, not to mention everybody we know praying for him," the rant hanging in the air.

"God will find a way," Paul gently said. "He brought me out of the darkness and gave me a reason for living when I had given up on myself. I'm sure He'll lift up that buddy of ours and put him back to work where he belongs."

The street lights lit up the main street of Houghton as Paul crossed the lift bridge to take Jenny home.

CHAPTER 9

Paul noticed a light on inside the kitchen as he pulled up in front of the Mission to unload the van.

"Anybody home," he shouted as he unlocked the front door and entered the building.

"I'm not so sure I'd call this a home," Del said sticking his head around the corner of the kitchen.

Del Souter, most recently from the coal mining area of Eastern Kentucky, and newly appointed afternoon shift director of the Hancock Youth Mission was sitting at a picnic table in the kitchen counting out change from the pop and candy concession machines. Del was a master banjo picker, first rate carpenter, and college apartment refurbisher, not to mention a newly converted member of the local Community Christian Church.

"It looks like we made enough money today to open up another satellite youth mission," Paul said.

"Definitely a thirsty, hungry bunch," Del responded.

"How's the man?" Del asked as Paul pulled up a chair.

"Jenny says his legs are on the mend, but he's still torturing himself inside about the accident."

"Any thoughts on when he'll be back?"

"Nothing specific, but we can hope."

"And pray," Del added.

Del swept all of the money into a cloth bag and put it in the wall safe.

"I'm gonna slip over and say good night to Fiona," Del said. "I think she's feeling kind of neglected since I started running the night shift here at the Mission."

"You head on over and sing her one of those mountain love songs your so good at. I think that'll do the trick."

"Ain't no trick at all," said Del putting on his jacket, "just pure mountain magic."

Fiona Devitt, a foreign exchange student from Northern Ireland, was a scholarship student at Finlandia University in Hancock, and earned extra money tutoring students on the violin. She and Del had become the talk of the town after playing at the Sunday night services at the Community Church. Their only commitment was to the next song, whatever that might be.

CHAPTER 10

Her name was Juanita Ortiz and she wasn't very tall, even for her age which was about two years old. But what she lacked in height God had over compensated her with curiosity and charm. She had been abandoned, or maybe just a victim of a bad decision of a frightened mother, but she was at least for the time being, tangled in a wool blanket in an upstairs bedroom, itchy, thirsty, and wondering where her mom was. This was not an unusual situation but she was too young to appreciate her predicament.

The muffled laughter from an area somewhere downstairs was keeping her awake, and her inability to figure out why her mom wasn't lying next to her made her sad, and scared.

Early the next morning Juanita heard a car horn and reached over to feel her mom's warm body, but the bed was cold; unslept in. The sunlight sneaking under the drawn window shade and slashing across her bed spread, announced a new day. With the faint noise of pots and pans being put to good use in the kitchen, she made her way down the dark stairs to the main floor clad only in her pajama bottoms and her favorite Tinkerbell Tee shirt.

"Buenos Dias, Senora," she said softly to Flora Gomez, a matronly looking Latina browning chorizo and onions in a cast iron skillet. There was a stack of flour tortillas wrapped in Aluminum foil warming in the oven next to a bowl of heuvos rancheros. The aroma permeating the entire house had her husband and three children salivating in anticipation of diving into this tasty Mexican breakfast.

Juanita slowly walked up to one of the two empty chairs, and looking at the dour face on the older man at her left, climbed up.

"Did she come home last night?" The man asked in English, knowing the little girl wouldn't understand him.

"Not yet," the mother quietly responded, turning to the oven to serve up the sausages and onions.

"I should never have permitted them into my home," he pontificated, looking around the table at his children, and then down at the little refugee.

"Papa," the woman whispered, "not in front of the child. She understands more than she lets on."

Oscar with that 'I told you so' look on his face took the bowl of eggs from Flora and served up the four little girls. The meal was eaten in silence and the littlest one ate the meat and a tortilla, and pushed the rest of the food around her plate. Everyone at the table left for their day's tasks while the youngest daughter cleared the table and did the dishes.

"Don't worry little one," she said to Juanita still sitting at the table. "She'll come back."

Juanita smiled at the young girl without understanding, but knowing. She then climbed down from the chair and quietly went back up to her bedroom. She and her mom Eva had responded to a recipe card posted on a cork board, in the front hall of a local down town community church. Things had fallen apart between Eva Ortiz and her last boyfriend and once again she was searching for her brother and dropping in on familiar social institutions to get her and Juanita off the street. She had to admit that Juanita was a pity magnate for big hearted church folks. A woman in the office at the church said that a Latino family in their congregation had an extra bed room for a young single woman. The card didn't mention children, but she knew Juanita's smile would get them in the door.

All morning long Juanita sat on the edge of the bed playing with the window shade cord waiting for the sound of her mother's foot steps running up the stairs. By lunch time Flora called the Downtown Community Church office, and explained the situation.

"I'm just concerned for the child," she explained to Marla Johnson, a part of the volunteer office staff.

"I'll call Angie Hendricks, the Pastors wife," Marla said. "Maybe she'll have an idea."

Angie was just finishing up helping the Hydro-therapist with Johnny when she heard her phone ringing in her purse at the other end of the therapy pool.

"Hi Marla, what's up?"

"You know the Gomez family who sit about ten rows back on the left hand side," Marla said using the international way of describing congregants in big churches.

"Man with a brush mustache, and three daughters," Angie responded as if the family picture in the church directory was unnecessary.

"Well, Flora, that's the mom, is part of the 'Help a Neighbor' program that the Women's Club sponsors and she took in a young mother and her two year old daughter. Anyway, her mother didn't come home last night and little Juanita is sitting in her bedroom all by herself. So…"

"Marla have you got Flora's phone number handy?" Angie asked grabbing a pen and note pad from her purse.

As wife of the head Pastor in a large city church, Angie's role was specifically undefined, and once again she was the quickest go between to help an unusual situation get some resolution.

"Hi, I'd like to speak with Flora Gomez, this is Angie Hendricks."

"Hello Mrs. Hendricks, this is Flora. I'm sorry to bother you, but we have a problem here, and the woman at the church said you might have some advice."

"Flora, if it's alright with you I could stop by your house. I'm downtown already and we could talk face to face."

Flora gave Angie her address, and then went upstairs to check on Juanita. The Gomez residence was in an older well kept neighborhood typical of the varied ethnicities scattered around the greater Grand Rapids area. As Angie climbed the front steps, a tiny nose was pressed up against the front door screen.

"Ola Juanita," Angie said smiling and bending down to greet her new little friend.

Juanita demurred staring at her bare toes.

Angie took the little girls hand and was led into the living room.

"Where's your Mama?" Angie asked Juanita in Spanish.

The child just stared at her. It was as if she had a million things to say but couldn't or wouldn't. She had that cold street wise look on her face that the two adults had seen many times before.

"Who wants a cookie and a cup of coffee?" Flora asked Angie breaking the silence.

"That would be wonderful," said Angie as they walked toward the kitchen.

On the way, Angie excused herself and called her husband at his office in the church.

"How's Johnnie?" He asked casually.

"Today was a good day. He seems to be getting his balance back and loves playing catch with the beach ball, but that's not why I'm calling," she said.

"I'm all ears," John responded.

Angie told him about the call from Flora and that Juanita was upstairs taking a nap.

"Hmm," the Pastor said mulling over the situation. "Let me call you back in a few minutes. I need to talk to a couple of people." He said goodbye and hung up. His next call was to the church legal council.

"Jimmy, its John Hendricks, have you got a minute?"

"You're the boss Pastor, fire away."

With the limited amount of information John was privy to, Jimmy wasn't prepared to make a judgment on the church's position regarding the child.

"I think the first thing we need to do is to make the child comfortable and find the mother. I'm not even sure where to start. I mean anyone who consciously leaves a two year old child with strangers is either irresponsible, or cruel," the lawyer said.

"Or frightened, or in trouble," added John. "I'm heading over to meet our little mystery girl. I'll be in touch," said John ending the call.

"Still no news?" John asked Angie entering Flora's house.

"Still a little girl without a mom," Angie replied.

"Good Morning Pastor," Flora smiled weakly, feeling a responsibility for this complicated situation.

"How are you Flora? It's nice to see you in spite of the circumstances."

"Do you have any guesses where we might start looking for a wayward mother?" He asked.

"No," she said, "and Oscar called a few minutes ago and wanted to call the police and have them come and pick up the child. He's very angry at the young mother who has put our family in this position. I told him that Angie was here, and that you were on your way, and that calmed him down a little. Really Eva, that's the mother's name, is not much more than a child herself," Flora said to no one in particular as she sat down on the couch with her hands in her lap, totally frustrated.

"Well, let's meet this little angel," John said. "Maybe she can help us figure this out."

"Juanita," Flora called up the stairs.

No answer.

"Juanita, ven aqui, por favor."

"Maybe she's fallen asleep," Angie suggested.

"I'll go wake her up and bring her down," Flora said. "It won't take a minute."

They could hear Flora rummaging from bed room to bed room calling Juanita's name.

"She's not up here," Flora said rushing down the stairs. "She's got to be around here somewhere."

"Flora, the back door is open!" Angie yelled from the kitchen.

"Maybe she went outside," she said with fear creeping into her voice.

John ran out the front door and circled the house. After walking down the street in both directions and calling out Juanita's name, he rushed back in through the front door of Flora's house and called the police.

"My name is John Hendricks and I need help searching for a missing little girl."

"Mr. Hendricks, give me your location, and a description of the child," said the desk sergeant.

John gave them the address and shouted to Flora for a description of Juanita. Before he could hang up, the sirens and flashing lights of a squad car pulled up in front of the house. Neighbors came out on their porches and met in the middle of the street drawn to the police car in dreaded anticipation. What was normally a quiet residential neighborhood had become ground zero, but nobody knew what was going on. Both ends of the block were cordoned off by police cruisers as the initial responders made their way to the front porch of Oscar and Flora Gomez' home.

"Sir we have the immediate neighborhood surrounded, and two dog units working their way towards the house even as we speak. We will find her Sir," the confident young officer promised.

"Maybe you should bring one of those K-9 teams into the house and make a thorough search first," suggested Angie.

"John, bring Rex down to the primary residence and search the home first," the police officer radioed to an officer a block away.

"On our way," the dog handler replied over the police radio.

Moments later another cruiser with a cage in the back pulled along side of the first responder. An older black officer approached the porch with a large dark brown and black German shepherd on a short leash. The K-9 Officer introduced himself to Flora and entered the home with the dog. Through the screen door, Flora suggested they try the first bedroom on the left at the top of the stairs. Rex clamored up the stairs with his nose to the carpet, made an immediate left turn and ended up with his snout and paw scratching at the comforter piled on the floor at the foot of the bed.

"Mrs. Gomez," the officer shouted down the stairs, "I think we've got something."

"Flora and her entourage rush into the bed room just in time to see a small hand reach out from under the spread and pet 'Rex the wonder dog's nose. Rex stood and returned to the officer's side as Flora lifted the bed cover and found Juanita scrunched in a little ball hiding her face from the light. Flora smiled and lifted the child into her arms. Juanita wrapped her arms around Mrs. Gomez. Juanita looked over Flora's shoulder at all of the strangers in the room, and ducked back down when she saw Oscar enter with a scowl on his face.

"What the...? Oh hello Pastor Hendricks," Oscar said catching himself in what might have been an impropriety in front of his minister.

"Good Morning Oscar," John said with a smile. "You're just in time to celebrate the return of our prodigal child."

"I'm not sure I see a whole lot of similarity between a foolish son and an abandoned little girl," Oscar said, "but at least we've solved half the problem. Now where is the little girl's mother?" He groused, looking at Flora.

You could see the embarrassment and irritation on Oscar's face. His chance to show Pastor John and Angie a quiet pleasant family home had been taken from him by the incorrigible mother of this child. His family would be the talk of their church. A church he and his family had tried so hard in which to make a good impression.

"Would you like to fill out a missing persons report?" The young officer standing behind Oscar asked.

"Maybe it's time to go down stairs, dismiss the posse, and figure out what we've got and where we go from here,"

John advised hoping to defuse the situation and calm Oscar down.

"That's a great idea Pastor," said Flora, "I'll go down and make some coffee."

"I'll help," offered Angie as the two women and Juanita made their way down stairs.

The policeman released his search party and contacted the Main Police Station with the details. The truant mother had not been gone long enough to warrant a missing persons report, but a 'be on the lookout advisory' had been authorized.

"So what do we do now?" Oscar asked the four other adults and the little girl who had somehow made her way onto Angie's lap sitting on the sofa next to Flora.

"Maybe we could…" started Flora.

"Maybe we could nothing," blurted out Oscar in a tone Flora had heard many times.

The room was quiet for a few moments. Juanita put her arms around Angie's neck and burrowed her head into her shoulder away from the adults, especially Oscar.

Running her fingers through the beautiful tresses of the child's long black hair brought back a memory from Angie's past.

"You know, my younger sister Maria couldn't have been much older than your mama when she and I walked through the border station at Tijuana those many years ago," she said looking at the child realizing that although Juanita was responding, she had no idea what Angie was saying.

"It was hot that day as we climbed onto a bus headed for San Diego knowing we might never see our family again. It was such an adventure; a scary adventure. My brother Jose and a friend left for Ciudad Juarez to cross into the United States at El Paso, Texas at the same time. We never heard from them again," she said absently to no one, "they just disappeared; gone."

Juanita stared up into the cheerless face.

"My sister and I, with help from friends and family made it all the way to Grand Rapids where I met John. Times were different then," she said looking at Flora. "We were treated poorly, but we weren't hunted like fugitives," she said with a scowl. "Don't worry," she said holding Juanita in front of her. "We will find your mama."

"She will stay here until we find Eva!" Flora said, staring daggers at her silent husband.

CHAPTER 11

The first Sunday in June was the kind of morning you dream about in February when you don't even want to get out of bed. Flowers blooming, birds singing, and a smile on every up turned face as the congregants entered the Downtown Community Church. The choir was singing Morning Has Broken, as Pastor John Hendricks entered the sanctuary through a side door, smiled at the organist, and took his seat behind the pulpit. Flora and the girls were seated in their usual spot, but for the second week in a row Oscar was not in attendance. He looked over in the other aisle and noticed that Angie was missing too. She was probably in the nursery reading a Spanish children's book to Juanita, he thought. The missing person's report on Eva had been filed a week ago, but there was nothing new from the local police. Child well fair services were now involved, and with Flora and Angie taking full responsibility for Juanita, there remained a rather tenuous status quo.

After opening with a prayer of welcome and current announcements, Pastor John opened his Bible to the Book of Luke and read the scripture of the Good Samaritan. The congregation then stood and sang Faith of our Fathers, followed by announcements, and the congregational offering. As the sanctuary quieted down, the Pastor stood behind the pulpit and told the story of Eva Nobody.

"This is all the information I have," he said to a hushed congregation. "There is a young woman, living or dead, in this community or maybe somewhere else, who longs for her only daughter, or hopes that she is in a better situation, and wants to return to her, or can't." John stood silently.

"Not much to go on, is it? We know who the child is. She's in the nursery at this very moment, hopefully with a drink box and someone to comfort her. If I had a picture of the mom, I would put it in the newspaper, or on every church bulletin board in the Grand Rapids area," John paused for a moment. "Once again in our daily lives we have reached the point where all we can do is throw up our hands or fall to our knees and ask God to give us a little more; a little more information, a little more hope, another do-over. Is Eva or her circumstances unusual in today's world? Is this huge problem of social and cultural disassociation between ourselves and our neighbor's just part of the ebb and flow of our daily lives which we as busy citizens have become numb to. After all, what can we do? We've got our own problems." John paused and looked around the Sanctuary. "Maybe this is the one that gets away from us. Maybe this is the one that fades away in our memories as explosions of future information and life's challenges push this event to the back of our memories. Is that all that's left for Juanita? Is she just another…?" John paused unable to finish the thought.

The congregation shuffled restlessly and stared at their hands as a hush enveloped the flock.

"If you have any thoughts or ideas that will help us find Eva and make this a better time for our little sister in Christ, please contact me. It can only make things better."

The organist played the opening strains of 'Abide With

Me' as the faithful rose and began singing the ageless hymn. Upon its conclusion, John stood, approached the pulpit, and asked the Lord to direct his words and thoughts and began his homily on the need to be our brother's keeper.

"But what if the answer is no? You ask. What if in spite of all we try to do or all we pray for, the desired outcome is beyond us?"

The pastor paused looking out over the throng.

"Worse yet, what if there is no answer at all. What if in spite of all we pray for and everything we do, there is no answer at all."

John bowed his head followed by the faithful,

> *"Dear Lord, sometimes all we know, and think we understand is not enough. So often the smugness we show on the outside is just a way of covering up the fear and uncertainty on the inside and we cry out to you expecting an answer, or the wisdom of that still small voice to make everything new. When it works we say thank you Lord, as if we have something to do with the outcome; as if You are some kind of a lucky medallion, a magic solution to use when things don't go our way. Why is it when things are unattainable, we hand it to You in prayer and unburden ourselves of any liability when perhaps we are the best hope. Open our hearts and minds to focus on the recovery of this missing young woman, and bring her home to this helpless child, Amen."*

John stood next to Angie holding Juanita's hand at the rear of the church as the parishioners made their way to the

Fellowship Hall. He thanked each person for worshiping with him this morning, and Juanita did all she could to smile and join in the hand shaking. The smiles were bitter sweet as friends and neighbors bent down to shake her tiny hand.

Jim Briggs, one of the ushers, came up to John and handed him a note. "This was in the bottom of one of the collection plates when we turned them in for counting."

John unfolded the offering envelope. Scratched on the paper was a semi-literate scrawl, 323 Brig Stret, upstars. John showed the note to Angie.

"Somebody knows something," he said.

"Wait," Angie said taking his arm, "before we go charging into somebody's home, maybe we'd better check first."

John nodded, shaking the last few hands.

Angie took Juanita to Flora and she, John, and Jim Briggs went out the side door to the Pastors car.

"Now I assume the Brig Stret, is Bridge Street across the river, but we've no way of even knowing for sure," John said as they all buckled up.

"Do you think we should get the police or child protective services involved?" Angie asked.

"Let's just see if there is such an address before we get too many people excited," John said cautiously, hoping that something good might come of this.

As urban neighborhoods go, the Bridge Street area went from an elitist history a hundred yeas ago of urban wealth, to disrepair and squalor with many generations in between. It's most recent resurrection came by way of an infusion of college students from Grand Valley State University as well as the entrepreneurial element of the youth movement in western Michigan. These young organizers bought and refurbished the many old buildings into campy little apartments and coffee shops to attract the hip and the curious.

The area was crowded with after church traffic in the restaurants and the regular locals drinking coffee and doing the Sunday Grand Rapids Press cross word puzzle at the side walk tables. John found a parking spot a half block away, and the three began checking addresses. Wading through busy sidewalk cafes, they found a 325 and a 321, but no 323. There was only a small taco shop with nine hungry customers waiting in line. Angie tried to talk to the cashier, but the customers weren't interested in her problems, and let her know it. It appeared that they had the wrong address when Jim came up and said there was an alley on the side of the building with a walk-up entrance.

"Let's give it a try," John said with little enthusiasm.

The pavement of the alley was slick with grease and grime from the taco restaurant, and the heat from the sun made the rancid smell almost unbearable. Five rickety wooden steps with no hand railing led up to a windowless door.

"Should we knock?" Jim asked having taken the responsibility of being the first one up.

Angie just shrugged her shoulders, and Jim rapped on the door hoping it wouldn't collapse.

No response.

"Try the handle," John said thinking it might be a storage area or ware house.

The handle turned and opened into a small hallway with another set of steps going up into darkness.

"Hello," shouted Angie feeling a little foolish.

The sound of scurrying feet interrupted the silence and the three looked at each other.

"Might be rats," John said, "Better be careful."

"Let me take a look," said Jim as he kicked through some news papers on the landing and started up the dark steps.

"Be careful," Angie said softly wondering why she was whispering.

"I hear a baby crying," said Jim turning back down towards the light.

Angie ran around him to the top of the stairs, and in the darkness shouted "Eva, I have Juanita and she needs you."

There was a moment of silence followed by a door opening down the hallway.

"No you don't," shouted a defiant voice approaching Angie.

"No, not here Eva," Angie said in a calming voice. "She's okay. She's with Mrs. Gomez at church, but she needs her mama."

Eva looked down the hallway. "Who are they?" She challenged pointing towards John and Jim.

"They are your friends. They are not the police."

"I want my daughter," Eva fired back.

"Come, we'll take you to her," Angie said sensing a little trust.

"Uno momento," Eva said returning to her room.

The conversation behind the door was loud but Angie was able to understand the conversation between Eva and a male companion. When the door opened, she came out holding the hand of a cautious young man.

"This is my brother Juan Ortiz," she said in English. "He is my brother and Juanita's uncle."

Standing on the stairs, John looked at Jim with a confused look on his face.

"It's a pleasure to meet you Juan, my name is Angie. Are there anymore of your family here?"

"No Senora," he said timidly. "There are just the two of us."

"Please come with us," Angie begged. "We'll pick up Juanita and find a better place to figure this out."

The two ducked back into the room and returned with two grocery bags full of old clothes and a couple of dirty blankets.

"Are we in trouble?" Juan asked John from the back seat.

"Did you do anything to get you in trouble?" John countered.

"I don't think so," Juan answered timidly.

The rest of the trip was uneventful. The five returned to the church, dropped off Jim and collected Juanita from Flora. Jim promise secrecy, and as John pulled away from the church, Flora gave Eva a very unchristian like look.

"Who was that man?" Eva asked.

"A friend from church who helped us find you," Angie said.

"I don't think I like him," Eva said.

John called Dutch with their pending arrival and realized that after today, the Hendricks family's life would be a little more interesting.

৯৯

"Well what have we got here?" Dutch said opening the back door.

"Dad I'd like to introduce you to Juanita's mom Eva and her brother Juan," John said helping with the bags.

"The pleasure is mine," said Dutch shaking Juan's hand, and smiling at Eva.

Angie explained that Dutch was her husband John's father and that both men were pastors of churches in Grand

Rapids. She added that Juanita was already staying with them.

You could tell by the look on Eva's face that she was not used to being around strong male figures.

After they had all settled in the living room and some lemonade had been poured, Angie said, "You are all welcome to stay with us until we can figure out a better plan."

Juan and Eva looked at each other in surprise.

"Why?" Eva said abruptly.

"Why not?" Angie parried.

"Well we don't even know you," said Eva.

The three Hendricks' looked at each other in shock.

"Did you know anybody in that filthy warehouse you were sleeping in while your daughter was crying for you," attacked Dutch.

"We don't need nothin from nobody!" spat back Eva and started to rise up off the sofa.

"Whoa, slow down. Let's start over, okay?" John offered with his hands in the air. "I think we can all figure this out if we all put our guns away, okay?"

"I'm sorry, and I'd like to apologize for my sister," Juan said. "We've been through some rough times lately and we're just not used to trusting people. It's not your fault, it's ours. So maybe this isn't such a good idea."

"There's only one concern in this room right now and that's how to help the little girl sitting next to her mom," John said gently. "Does anyone disagree?"

The six adults were a little embarrassed by the situation they had just created.

"Please let me apologize for my harsh words to you Eva," Dutch said. "It's been a long time since I've been in and around the care of babies, and I'm afraid I'm not the most qualified person in the room to lead a discussion on the best solution for making a better world for Juanita, but I will be more than grateful for an opportunity to help in any way I can," Dutch said.

"Thank you Dad," said John. "When we all get to know each other I'm sure we'll all make a great team. I think the biggest problem we have is that none of us has eaten much today and it's hard to be nice on an empty belly, agreed?"

They all smiled and Angie said," Dutch put a roast beef dinner in the oven when he got home from his church, and I'm sure that's what that wonderful smell is. Eva will you help me set the table please."

While the girls laid out the dinner, John and Juan carried the soiled clothes down to the laundry room, and got the wash started. Dutch sat with Juanita and read her a children's book. Eva stuck her head into the living room to watch the older and the younger generation enjoying each other's company and she approved.

As they settled around the dining room table, Dutch said, "In our home we always thank God for the many blessing that He shares with us, and today is extra special to have the Ortiz family as our guests. Will you bow your heads please?" Juanita stared at the apparent sleeping adults.

> *"Dear Lord it never ceases to amaze me that your love and grace always seems to triumph over our human short comings. We know that by living your Word we can create a better day for Juanita. Thank you for the meal placed before us and allow it to nourish our bodies in service to you, Amen."*

Juan and Eva gobbled down their dinner like they hadn't eaten in three days, which was probably the case.

After dinner a more productive discussion was held, and an informal agreement became an opportunity; an opportunity that seemed to please everyone.

"I know you would like to clean up, so if you will follow me and Juanita, we will show you your rooms," Angie said. "I'm sure our son Johnny won't mind lending you some of his clothes," Angie said smiling at Juan, "and Eva I've got some things that will fit you."

John took Juan to a spare bed room in the basement while Eva settled into the room where Juanita slept. An hour later with clean bodies and fresh clothes they all settled around the dining room table again for some home made strawberry shortcake.

"We don't mean to pry," Angie said, "but anything you can tell us might help to straighten things out. Was that your home Juan?"

The two teens smiled at each other and Juan said, "Who could possibly live in a terrible place like that?" He said wiping the whipped cream from his mouth.

There was a relieved chuckle from the Hendricks.

"Did I hear a baby crying down the hall where you were staying last night?" John asked.

"Yes," said Eva. "They moved in last night. We only just met them this morning."

"How old is the baby?" Angie asked.

"Not too old," said Eva. "She has a terrible cough. I think she needs help."

John looked at Dutch.

❧

At 6:00 P.M. Sunday evening, John called an emergency meeting of the church council to discuss their options. The seven member panel was made aware of the current situation with Eva and Juan, and also the peril of the young family in the ware house on Bridge Street.

"Maybe we should call the police?" Barb Hoch suggested, "Just to be safe."

"I'm not sure this is a legality issue. I mean I don't think anyone has broken any laws, or if they have, we certainly aren't aware of them," said Jim Briggs.

"Maybe we should appoint a team to go and investigate the situation," said Terry Quinn.

Dutch who was sitting at the end of the table as a visitor said, "If that was your daughter and grandchild lying in that filth right now, what would you do?"

"We just rescued Juanita's family," John with conviction, "can we do any less for these poor souls?"

John reached for his phone, and called Angie.

"Hi Hon, we've decided to try and rescue the other family in the Taco warehouse. Can you grab Juan and meet us there to help with the translating?"

"We'll be there in twenty minutes," she said. "Wait for us, and be careful."

John dismissed the council and promised to keep them informed. He took Dutch and Jim and drove back to the alley off Bridge Street to wait for Angie and Juan. There was a party atmosphere in the sidewalk cafes around the corner as the three men sat in the car with the sky darkening; each with their own thoughts.

"You know we might get them all deported," Jim said.

No one spoke.

"I mean, I know we're all trying to help, but …"

"Jim, I wish I had the answer for how to make things right, but as simplistic as it sounds, we've got to leave it in God's hands."

"If we do nothing else, we've got to get that baby to a doctor," Dutch said. "If we don't, we are playing God with a defenseless soul. I don't want that on my conscious."

The headlights of a car turned into the alley and pulled up behind John. Angie and Juan approached with flashlights in hand.

"I think this will come in handy so we don't break our necks on those stairs," Angie said.

"How do you want to do this?" John asked.

"I think if Juan and I go up alone it will be less frightening for the family. Juan had a conversation with them this morning and they were pretty nervous. I just hope the baby's all right," Angie added.

The beams from the flashlights danced off the walls and ceiling as they made their way up the dark stairway accompanied by the loud beat of a guitar bass from a rock band at a nearby night spot. There was little fresh air to breathe as the daytime heat had turned the warehouse into a pressure cooker.

"That poor baby has to be heat stressed, although I don't hear any crying," she whispered.

As they walked down the hallway single file, there wasn't a sound coming from any of the rooms. Juan pointed to a room up on the left.

"Paco, Its Juan Ortiz from across the hall, are you all right?"

No sound.

"Paco, it's me Juan let me in."

Juan tried the door knob and entered with no resistance. The place was like an oven, but nobody was there. The smell of dust and sweat were over powering. Juan shined the flashlight around the tomblike room, but they were gone, along with any belongings they might have had. The only sign that they had ever existed was a tiny rag with what looked like dried blood laying in the filth. Juan could hear Angie whispering a prayer behind him. They both backed out and quietly closed the door.

There was almost a chill in the air as they exited the building. The three men declined the invitation to inspect the room, and the five leaned on John's car in silence tormented by a lost opportunity. John stopped a patrol car driving by and explained the situation, and the officers said they would check it out, but the officers explained that in this part of town, vagrants, indigents and poverty was part of their daily routine as they performed their duties. John called it in to the station, took Jim back to the church and went home. Angie and Juan drove around the neighborhood looking for any sign of the family and after a couple of hours, they went home too. It was like a death in the family.

CHAPTER 12

"Hey show off," Mary said entering the therapy room and watching Johnny walking with the aid of the parallel bars.

Johnny looked up with a sweat towel wrapped around his neck, and jokingly asked, "Did you bring me my car keys?"

"I'm not sure you're ready for that, but you're getting closer," she answered.

The progress Johnny was making was remarkable. The combination of space age therapy equipment and the competence of his experienced staff had taken this suffering hulk and turned him back into the Johnny of old. Even the spider web of anger he was carrying around inside of him since the accident was dissipating through counseling and family reinforcement. Doctor Phillips and his staff were removing the demons Johnny had been carrying around for years, and it appeared that there was light at the end of the tunnel. That light was the God that he had rejected and found again. Dutch had told Johnny that God had never left him. He had left God.

"God loves you and he will always wait for you to come home to Him," Dutch had said on a particularly bad night a few weeks ago. Now Johnny was proud of what he had accomplished and humbled by the selfish attitude that had brought him down. With this new enthusiasm he was determined to get back up to Hancock and continue to do the work that God had chosen for him; the sooner the better.

"Keith and I would like to have you and your family out to our home in Rockford this coming Saturday for a barbeque. Your mom has already accepted, how about you?" Mary asked.

"I don't have a thing to wear," he teased with the biggest smile Mary had seen in weeks.

The invitation had been made weeks before, but he didn't think he would ever get out of his wheel chair. Now the reality of regaining his old life was almost more than he could imagine. He still had flashback images of that snowy day in February when his life changed forever. The image of Bob Rogers, his new, and now deceased friend still haunted him. The lesson that he had to learn was how to forgive himself and accept the fact that he was not responsible. The knowledge that God had a plan helped him to put it all into perspective. He also had to accept that he was not the reason for the positive good things that had happened in the last six months. He was only a small part of God's plan; a very small part. That was probably the biggest lesson of all. *Do what you can and give God the glory,* he thought quietly with a smile on his face. It seemed so easy now.

"Why are you smirking?" Mary asked.

"Just a little joke between me and God," he said.

"Well good," she said closing the subject. "We'll expect you all at 2:00 Saturday afternoon."

Angie called Mary's mom a few days before the picnic and told her about their new house guests.

"Betty I've got the craziest story," she said, "and I've got to tell somebody."

"I'm all ears," Betty Vander Meer said.

Angie recounted the story of Juanita coming into their lives, and finally finding Eva and Juan.

"Life was moving almost faster than we could deal with it. We continued to search for the Paco family." She explained. "We called them that because Juan and Eva never learned their last name before they just disappeared. We even tried the hospitals. Anyway, Juan and Eva were both quiet for a few days and we wondered if they might be thinking about running too."

"You've got to be kidding," Betty said.

"Now this will really blow your mind," Angie said getting in the spirit of the conversation with her new friend.

"The third day she's there in our home, Eva comes up to me and says she wants to call her mother."

"No!" Betty said in astonishment.

"To be polite," I asked, "where does your mother live?"

"Chicago," she said, and both women started giggling.

"What part of Mexico is that?" said Bette bursting into laughter.

"By the way, come to find out Eva and Juan are actually from New Mexico. They're not illegal, there just on the run. Their mother left her husband down in some border town and moved to Chicago to live with her sister."

"You've got to be kidding," Betty repeated herself.

"You know, in spite of how crazy it sounds, it's almost the story of my own life," Angie said quietly in a sobering tone, "except I was the real runaway."

The conversation stalled and Betty quietly asked, "Angie are you all right?"

Through sniffles and tears, Angie once again recounted her odyssey to a woman she had never met.

Saturday was one of those rare summer days with cloudy skies and low humidity; a perfect day for a picnic. John and Dutch had stopped at Mary Free Bed to pick up Johnny, and together with Angie and the Ortiz clan drove to Rockford and pulled into Keith's driveway.

Keith, Mary, and their two year old daughter Amy stood on the front porch with her folks Dick and Betty sitting on the glider.

Introductions were made. Hand shakes, smiles, and hugs were exchanged and everyone made their way to the back deck. Betty put her arm around Angie as if they were old friends. It pleased both women that God had pulled them together during a difficult time.

Taking over as host, Dick announced that he had lemonade, ice tea, and a little left over breakfast coffee. Betty set up the drinks while Amy took Juanita's hand and led her to the backyard followed by an aging Corky.

"You have a beautiful daughter," Mary told Eva.

The two mothers sat in the grass and watched Amy play the big sister role in the sand box.

"I've known Angie and John for a couple of months now. This must be a big adjustment for all of you," Mary said.

"I don't know where we'd be if it wasn't for the Hendricks family. Dutch is really good with Juanita too. He reads her stories before bedtime every night," said Eva warming to Mary.

"Does she have grandparents?" Mary asked trying to make conversation.

"Just my mother," she replied. "My father lives in La Mesa, New Mexico just north of Juarez. It's a little hole in the wall suburb of Las Cruces on the main road to the Mexican border."

"What does he do there?" Mary asked.

"Not much, he hurt his back working in a tire repair shop. Now he just sits around and complains to anyone who will listen."

"So you and Juan just sort of travel around,"

"We came north looking for work, but so far no one will pay us enough to get a place to live."

"What about you're Mom?"

"She cleans motel rooms with her sister," she paused, "and they don't need anymore mouths to feed."

"Did you finish High School?"

Eva nodded.

"What would you like to do?"

"Anything, we're tired of running and being broke."

"Let me get you some more lemonade," Mary said standing and walking towards the house. The reality of Eva and Juan's life choices made Mary grateful that God had given Keith and her a greater purpose in life. It was all Corky could do to get up off his haunches and follow Mary up the steps to the rest of the family.

"Those young'uns seem to get along pretty well," said Johnny as Mary passed by.

"Kids have a way of figuring things out in a hurry," Mary replied. "You seem to have everything well in hand," she smiled, "I wish Jenny was here this afternoon."

"I do too," he said. "You know we've only been together less than a year, but I don't remember having a life before her."

"Have you told her that?"

"Well," he paused, "I think she knows that."

"You know everybody likes to be appreciated and not taken for granted." Mary opined.

"I hate to say it, but I've been so wrapped up in my own stupidity for so long that I'm sure I've been abusing everyone around me."

"Not exactly everyone," she joked, "but you could polish up your charm a little bit around those who think the world of you."

"You know you're absolutely right. I think I'll call Jenny and see how she's doing," he said reaching for his phone.

"Probably wouldn't do any harm," she said patting him on the shoulder and heading for the kitchen to get Eva some more ice tea.

"Is dat you baby?" he asked in his best gangster jargon.

"Who want's ta know," Jenny responded.

"The man that loves you more than anything else on earth," he said wiping a tear from his eye.

"Hang on Honey, it won't be much longer, I promise."

CHAPTER 13

Two weeks later, Dad pulled the brand new nine passenger van up to the front door of the hospital, where a line of trainers, therapists, doctors and friends lined both sides of the walkway as Johnny and Angie slowly walked through the gauntlet of love to the freedom he'd been looking for. Doctors' Van Every and Phillips were at the end of the line with broad smiles as Johnny approached them both with tears in his eyes.

"I love you both," he said embracing each of them.

"We love you too," said Dr. Van Every trying to look professional but not succeeding.

"You're not getting away from us that fast," said his psychiatrist.

"My best therapist will be knocking on your front door Monday morning for out-patient therapy, so don't get too comfortable at your parents home," Dr. Van Every joked. Johnny gingerly climbed into the front passenger seat and closed another chapter in his life.

"Pretty snappy van," Johnny said as they pulled away.

"I'm glad you like it," John said "because it belongs to you."

"You're kidding," Johnny said.

"No son, I'm afraid this was the best we could do with the money from the insurance company and the cash settlement from the county."

"Thank you Jesus," was Johnny's only response.

Dutch and some of the neighbors and church members from John's flock were standing on the sidewalk in front of the Hendricks house as they pulled into the driveway. The crowd stood in anticipation as the passenger door opened and a cane followed by two hesitant feet hit the concrete. Johnny paused for a moment and considered how much his life had changed since the last time he was here. He hoped that it wasn't too obvious that the positive, confident young man they had loved and grown to rely on was now full of self doubt and introspection.

"I hope I don't fall on my nose" he said to Angie in the back seat as he pushed off the door edge and pulled on his cane at the same time.

A cheer filled the air as he stood and caught his balance. Johnny looked around at the dozen smiling faces welcoming him back to a world in which he had lived most of his life. A tear slid down his cheek. He tried to speak, but no words were sufficient to express how he felt at the moment.

"Give him a little room friends," Dutch sided like a mother hen, as the entourage allowed Johnny his first steps of freedom.

"Well what do you think?" Angie asked seeing the indecision in his eyes.

He reached over and pulled his mom to him, and whispered, "I love you mom."

As he slowly made his way to the new ramp the church

men's group had built, he saw a familiar face sitting on the front porch. The Hendricks' flew Jenny down from Hancock the day before and put her up in the last spare bedroom. She made her way down the ramp never taking her eyes off of Johnny's, and carefully embraced him. She gently kissed him and whispered in his ear, "Long time no see stranger, I love you."

The love in his eyes said all that needed to be said.

John announced that there were refreshments in the back yard, and the retinue slowly made their way up the driveway to a group of church women standing behind plates of rolled sandwiches, pitchers of ice cold lemonade, and of course pies and cakes.

Johnny was offered a seat at the head of one of the tables as John asked everyone to take a seat. The group sat quietly expecting John to offer up Grace. John stood behind his son with his hands on Johnny's shoulders.

"Six months ago on a cold snowy Saturday night, we received a phone call from a doctor in Marquette," John said looking at his friends and neighbors. "The doctor said that our only son had been seriously injured in a horrific car accident but that he was still alive and was being flown from the Keweenaw to Marquette Hospital to try and save his life. I pray that none of you ever experience a call like that, and if you have, you know where our hearts were." John stopped for a moment and squeezed his son's shoulders, and with a husky voice continued. "What we found when we arrived in Marquette, was a young man with a broken body, and a broken spirit. What you see at the head of this table is a young man with a healing body and a soaring spirit thanks to the love of God and some wonderful people at the Mary Free Bed Hospital. Angie, Dad, and I are grateful for this healing as well as the prayers and good thoughts from all our friends and parishioners." John bowed his head,

> *"Father God, You are indeed the Great Physician and for that we give you all our thanks. Bless this food lovingly prepared by friends and family, and help it to strengthen our body's to help do your work and spread your love. Amen."*

For some inexplicable reason, everyone cheered and slapped each other on the back after the prayer, and John gave his son a careful bear hug. An hour later, the guest had left and John and Angie carried the left over's into the house while Dutch folded the chairs and tables and stowed them in the garage. It was still warm and pleasant in the back yard and Johnny and Jenny sat at the last table holding hands and enjoying each other's company.

"How do you really feel," she asked. "Are you okay?"

"Really?" He asked.

"Really, really," she said.

"Don't tell anybody, but I'm scared to death."

She reached over, pulled him close, and kissed him gently.

"That scares me too," he whispered in her ear.

"Johnny Hendricks how can I possibly scare you?" She asked.

"You don't scare me honey, it's just that I don't know if I can be the same Johnny who left Houghton all busted up." He started to tear up again.

Jenny wiped away a tear.

"Those sessions I had with Dr. Phillips left me doubting a lot of who I thought I was. The four months before the accident were kind of like a fairy tale. Everything seemed so easy. I can hardly believe it myself. If I told a stranger about all of the wonderful miracles that happened to us," he stopped. "Yes, they happened to all of us, he wouldn't believe me. But lying in that hospital bed I've never felt so alone, or so useless. It seemed like some one opened the door, kicked me out and the whole rest of the world went on without me. After you left it was even worse. I never want to spend another night in any hospital. I will forever have a new empathy for any patient I visit. I feel like I'm just running off at the mouth. Jenny I love you so much, and I'm so sorry I treated you so badly when you came so far to help me. I'm so ashamed," he said laying his head on her shoulder.

Jenny ran her fingers through his curly hair and sat quietly thanking God for this special moment.

The next few weeks in the Hendricks household were anything but normal. Johnny's therapist arrived every morning at 9A.M. and the stretching began. A small gym was set up in the basement with a treadmill and stationary bike. Mary Free Bed provided most of the stretching equipment as well as the free weights. Stacy Veenstra, a young athletic physical therapist from the Hospital's out patient department, met Jenny at the front door, and together they led Johnny down to his new torture chamber.

"The hard part is over," Stacy said. "The only thing left to do is take those muscles that have been taking a nap since the accident, and turn them back into big strapping muscles to make you stronger."

"Hmm," Jenny mused, "I don't remember any big strapping muscles before the accident."

"They were there. You just weren't looking very closely," said Johnny.

"Okay," she smirked, "If you say so."

Stacy quietly adjusting the tread mill winking at Jenny.

"Well maybe we can encourage those muscles to rise to the occasion," Stacy said joining in the repartee.

"I can see you two have got me outnumbered..."

"And outsmarted," Jenny added finishing the sentence.

"Okay, I give up," Johnny said throwing his hands in the air.

There was a determination he hadn't felt before as the three of them cross trained their bodies for the next couple of weeks.

Meanwhile, Dutch took advantage of Juan's availability and put him to work planting and pruning their much neglected backyard and garden. Eva, Angie, and Juanita visited the neighborhood municipal swimming pool each morning which taught free swimming lessons to the little ones.

As Juanita flapped her water wings, Eva and Angie got to know each other better.

"What was your specialty down in La Mesa, New Mexico when you were growing up?" Angie asked.

"What's a specialty?" Eva asked.

"You know, what did you like to do?"

"I don't remember liking anything. It seemed like everybody was just trying to get away. Even in school, there was no motivation to succeed at anything. We all knew we were just going to find a job and get married."

"I understand," Angie said, "that's why my sister and I left Mexico."

"Momma, look at me," Juanita shouted splashing water on a frightened little boy.

"You be nice to him," Eva shouted, but Juanita was having too much fun to care.

The little boy's mother gave Eva a knowing smile.

"You know John and I have been talking and praying about your situation as well as Juan's," Angie said. "I know it must be frustrating having so much responsibility and so little freedom to try and make a future for you."

"We don't have any responsibilities," Eva said, "we don't have nothing; no money, no home, no job," she paused with a hopeless look on her face.

"You do have two things going for you that I think are pretty special," Angie offered.

"And those are?" Eva challenged still feeling self pity.

"You have a God that loves you, and you have a daughter who deserves better than her mother had."

"I'm sorry, but I don't think God's too happy with the Ortiz family at the moment," she said lowering her head. "I think we kind of messed that up. When we were small, we went to mass every morning. Mamma was so proud of me and Juan. She used to brag that some day he might be a priest," she said wistfully.

"What happened?" Angie asked.

"Nothing happened," Eva shot back." That's the whole point, you keep waiting for that special something to happen, but it never does."

"Does Juanita have a daddy?" Angie asked, hoping she hadn't crossed the line.

"No," Eva said somberly, "at least nobody who wants to be. Juanita, you come over here and put on some more sun screen," she yelled, changing the mood and the subject. "You know even though our skin is darker, we've still got to protect it," she said to Angie, but Angie's mind was somewhere else.

☙

The following Sunday after church the Hendricks/Ortiz clan had a picnic in the back yard with Dutch in charge of the cooking. Everyone was in a light hearted mood. Johnny had spoken to the flock at his dad's church on the importance of self forgiveness after a tragedy, and the message was well received.

"You know son, I learned a lot from your presentation this morning. It's interesting how God can take a terrible experience in someone's life and turn it into a positive for that person as well as those around him."

"It seems like sometimes you've got be beaten over the head to make sense out of misery and injustice," Johnny said standing between his dad and grandpa at the barbeque grill.

"If God gave us all we needed to know to prepare us for our daily struggles at one time, I'm afraid it would be overwhelming. The Bible tells us to listen to that still small voice from the Holy Spirit to guide and direct us, and it isn't always easy to decipher the message," said Dutch.

"I'm not sure I would have made it through this last challenge if it weren't for my family," Johnny said to the two most important men in his life.

"If you don't change the subject," John said, "your grandpa's going to burn all the hot dogs."

Holding hands around the big picnic table, John prayed,

> *"Father God, we are constantly humbled by your wisdom and grace. Help us to be better stewards of the opportunities we are given, and thank you for this feast which we are about to partake in. Amen."*

Juanita, with a mustard covered face, smiled at Angie while stuffing a hot dog into her little mouth.

After lunch, Dutch and Johnny carried out the old croquet set from the garage and everyone but Juanita had a great time playing the game. She just sprawled on her back in the warm grass and watched the clouds roll by, just as God intended.

CHAPTER 14

That evening John met with Eva in his home office. "I know you're having a tough time trying to figure out what plans God has for you, and I think I might have an answer," he said with his hands folded over his chest. "This past Thursday evening at the church council meeting, one of our members asked how you and Juan were doing. I was surprised by the number of members in our group who showed an interest in your family and told similar stories about people in their lives. Some of the folks were family members; some were friends or neighbors. The point is Eva, you and Juan are not the only teenagers and early 'twenty-something's who feel lost and disenfranchised in this world we live in. I'm afraid my generation took it for granted that our nation's youth had everything they needed to become successful in this country. It seems no one bothered to ask how you were doing, or what your goals and dreams were. If you aren't born in the right economic environment or social stratum, the proper stepping stones needed to find your own way aren't always available." Having said that," he continued, "Talk is cheap."

Eva nodded her head without saying anything and wondered where this conversation was going.

"Our church is part of an assembly of faith based organizations whose job it is to find people like you and Juan, and match your skills and needs with opportunities in the greater Grand Rapids area. Now I know you're saying to yourself that you don't have any skills, but that's not true. You're young, ambitious, motivated, and probably most importantly, you're bi-lingual. Do you know how many jobs are available for someone who speaks Spanish and English fluently?"

"Yeah, but not for me," she demurred.

"And why not?" John asked.

"I'm just not good enough," she answered, looking at the ceiling.

"I'll tell you what," he paused, "If you will come with me tomorrow morning and take some tests, we will know more than we do right now, okay."

"Well…"

"If not for you, then how about doing it for Juanita," he badgered.

Eva toyed with a cuticle on her left hand. "I'm afraid," she said stoically.

"Life can be scary Eva. Repeat after me, me and God can do anything."

"What?"

"Me and God can do anything," he repeated.

"Me…"

"Me and God," he added.

"Can do anything," he finished. "Now say it again."

Eva repeated the Mantra two more times, and smiled.

"Get a good night sleep, because tomorrow we've got business to attend to."

"Number 18."

Eva looked down at the ticket she had pulled from the machine by the front door. The ticket read Number 19, and as she looked up, another bushy haired gangly teenager with a John 3:16 Tee shirt on and his jeans drooping down past his buns strolled up to the counter to be handed a test to fill out to tell him what his future would be. Eva looked around the room and sensed most of the bypassed generation frankly didn't care. The last two generations before them had been convinced that money and power were the goals and the only way to achieve these things were to follow the rules and follow the leader and hope you were selected for whatever. The young man at the counter smiled at the clerk, and ambled over to a chair with a desk top, plopped down and signed his name to a five page questionnaire to help somebody decide where he might fit in. The truth was, he was already in, and there really wasn't much he was interested in to take the place of his digs in his dad's basement, his phone and his video games.

"Number 19."

Eva approached a woman motioning towards her two counters down from Number 18. She could sense from the insincere smile on the woman's face that she had been dealing with people like Eva for most of her adult life.

"Are you here for the exam?" She said looking over Eva's shoulder.

"I think so," Eva replied.

"Name."

"Eva Maria Ortiz."

"Citizenship."

"American."

"Identification."

Eva rummaged through her rag purse knowing the only

I.D. she had was a lapsed drivers license from New Mexico with a three year old picture of her. She slid it towards the woman and knew that after a careful perusal the interview would be over.

"I'm sorry," said the disinterested woman handing her back her defunct driver's license, "please take a seat over on the wall, and some one will talk to you. Number 22," she said already focusing on the next opportunist.

Eva had used her driver's license on her way up from New Mexico, but this was different; this was something official. She had never been official before. Eva turned and walked out the front door.

Out on the street she phoned John.

"Well that was quick," the Pastor said. "What did they say?"

"They…, she…, she didn't say anything, I guess."

Silence.

"Are you still there?" John asked hearing the failure in her voice.

"This isn't going to work," she said cutting the connection and walking to a near by bench and sitting, hoping someone in a big truck would run over her and put her out of her misery.

"What'd they tell you?" Number 18 asked by way of introduction as he neared the loser's bench. It never dawned on either of them that they were part of a vast network of under achievers across the country going no where. Pastor John knew it. The clerk in the unemployment office knew it, but these two young American citizens were oblivious to the fact that they had been left behind without even knowing it.

"She never even got to the question," Eva said smirking defiantly.

"I don't see what the big deal is anyway," the young man

said. "They want you to get a job so you can get minimum wage and waste all your time working. By the way I'm Neal," he said.

John pulled up to the curb, tooted his horn, rolled down his window, and with a big smile said, "How 'bout some breakfast."

Eva left Neal and ran towards the car suddenly sensing that this preacher she had only recently met was on her side.

"Well that couldn't have been much fun," he said with a grin.

Eva relaxed. "No it wasn't," she simpered.

For the first time in a long time she felt like she had a friend who might understand.

༄

Later that evening listening to the chirp of the crickets, John, Angie, and Dutch sat out in the back yard looking up at the stars and cooling off from the day's heat.

"You know, maybe what we're trying to do isn't the answer," John said. "If running our young people through the established system was the path to get them back on track, the problem would have been solved by now and we wouldn't need the system."

"It's obvious that nothing works well for everyone," Dutch opined. "I'm sure that the job corps idea must work for the majority, but there are always some who are drawn in a different direction."

"Isn't that the way God works?" Angie asked, watching a shooting star streak across the sky. "Everyone has a destiny and a different path to fulfill it. If my sister and I hadn't got on that bus in Tijuana a long time ago, we wouldn't be having this conversation, would we."

"You sure would have missed out on a great guy," John joked.

Angie leaned over and gave him a rap on the head.

Early the next morning Johnny walked into the kitchen following the aroma of freshly brewed coffee.

"Good morning Sis," he said to Eva.

"Why do you call me Sis?" She asked.

"Because you're my sister in Christ," he said smiling.

"And I suppose you're my brother in Christ," she suggested.

"You got it Sis."

"Hmm"

"You want to go for a walk around the block?" He asked.

"If it will help you get stronger Bro," she said.

They were half way down the block when he asked, "What do you want to do?"

"Do you mean now?"

"No," he said earnestly, "I mean with your life."

There was silence as they kept walking.

"You know you're a lot like your dad," she said trying to change the subject.

"I consider that a complement."

"It was meant to be," she replied.

"Well."

"I don't know, but I can't stay here," she said stopping and turning to Johnny. "You have all been so kind to us, but this isn't where we belong. We have no roots here, and we need to find the right place. It's hard to explain. I'm not even sure I'll know it when I see it. We just have to keep looking." She started walking again. "I don't know how to tell your mom. She is so attached to Juanita, and Juan and Dutch have become 'brothers in Christ' as you say."

"I know God will show you the way," he said, "let's head back and see about some breakfast."

❧

Very early the next morning Johnny was lying in bed when he had a visit from that still small voice. It was so clear and distinct that he seemed to be awake.

It's time, the voice said. *You are ready, and your destiny awaits you. There is work to be done in the Keweenaw. Follow your heart. The Lord will lead you.*

Johnny jumped out of bed and began pacing the floor. He had things to do. It all became so clear that he was shocked that he hadn't seen the answer before. His vision was much bigger than the Mission, and all the of the people that God had put in his life in the last nine months suddenly fit into place in the grand scheme of things, and now was the time. He threw on his clothes and rushed down the hall to Jenny's room.

Tap, tap, tap. "Psst, Jenny," he whispered.

The door slowly opened and a sleepy Jenny asked, "Why don't you wake up the whole house?"

Johnny threw open the door, and shouted "we're going home."

Lights went on all over the house and everyone met in the kitchen bleary eyed and concerned.

Everybody else just stood there, or sat there and stared at Johnny who seemed to be on fire.

"Maybe with a little bacon and eggs and a cup of black coffee things will make a little more sense," Dutch suggested.

By the time breakfast was ready, Johnny was back in his room praying.

Things began happening quickly. Mary Free Bed gave

their okay with the condition that Johnny return for periodic check ups. He called The Mission and talked with Paul and Del, and told them he would soon be back in Pastyland to stay. He called Ernie Sugg and discussed a possibility he had in mind. He called Kertu Lehto to confirm some things.

Bob Heikenin was next on his list, and finally he called Helen Aho.

"Hello," she answered.

"Is this my landlady?" He asked.

"Johnny," she tearfully whispered, "is dat you."

"Is my room still available?"

"Of course it is," she said softly.

"Jenny and I are coming home."

"When?"

"Very soon," he said, "I'm back on my feet."

"Johnny," Helen said. "I love you and I'm glad you're all better."

"I love you too Helen," he said and hung up.

Later in the day he called Victor Wurtz.

"Is dis my favorite broom pusher?" Johnny asked.

"I taut I was da only broom pusher you knew," Victor responded.

"Are you kidding?" Johnny jested. "You're only my favorite; an important man like me has lots of custodial friends."

"I shoulda known," Victor said.

"I'm getting ready to head north, and I'm wondering how serious you are about going home."

There was silence on the other end of the line.

"How soon?" Victor asked.

"Maybe a week." Johnny said. "I'll call you again in a few days and we'll talk."

"Okay Johnny dat'll be good," and he hung up.

"Lord hold me tight and don't let me fall, Johnny Hendricks thought as he went down stairs whistling.

A few days later Johnny was prepared to share his vision.

"I know you're all wondering what's going on in that little addled brain of mine," he said to Dutch and his mom and dad at their favorite pizza restaurant. "You know I've spent the last six months wandering in the wilderness. I lost a friend, I lost my ability to function, and I lost my faith, and you've witnessed it all."

They all nodded in agreement.

"In retrospect, it was a perfect Hell. Who we are and where we're going is all we have. The foreseeable future is based upon our acceptance of our needs and desires, and I lost them all," he said reflectively. "But at some point in that haze of frustration and doubt, Grandpa told me a truth that I discarded until it was time to join the world again." Johnny looked at Dutch and said "God never leaves you; you leave God."

Patting his grandpa's hand Johnny said, "It seems so simple now, but in that haze of self pity and disgust, I forgot that the love of God was what put me on that mountain in the first place. It's a lesson I'll never forget."

"You know, it wasn't that long ago the four of us were a pretty good team," John said.

"And the three of us are ready to get on board again," Angie added.

"How can we help?" Dutch asked.

Johnny smiled. "You know I thought the mission in the Upper Peninsula seemed a little crazy when I mentioned it last year."

"It's never crazy when it's from your heart, and it's doing God's work," Angie said.

The three mentors' sat in anticipation.

Johnny began by reminding his family of his first excursion to the U.P. and all of the people he had met and become friends with. They recalled the series of events and outcomes which brought about a stronger community and eventually the Hancock Youth Mission on Quincy Street. He mentioned the solid bonds created between Dad's Central Community Church, Grandpa's Eastside Christian Reformed Church and the Houghton/Hancock Clergy Association. It was truly the Hand of God working through these organizations that helped resolve local problems in the Keweenaw communities, culminating with the jewel in the crown; the Mission and its outward reach to the youth in the area.

"I am humbled by what we have accomplished in such a short time, but, it took a young girl from New Mexico to make me realize that the problems we are facing cannot be cured by the Mission alone. No, that is only the beginning. When Eva walked into that unemployment agency here in Grand Rapids and didn't realize that she was already lost, and frankly didn't care, that's when the bells went off. The vision I had the other day woke me up to a larger problem, and funny enough, the last ten months of my life have placed me in a perfect position to do something about it."

"We're all ears," said Angie.

"The Keweenaw Peninsula is sort of a microcosm of the problems the whole United States faces," Johnny began. "It started out as a place to make money; in this case the copper industry. Once the profitability was passed down to the miners, the subsidiary businesses grew around the community like mushrooms. The need for shelter, food, and security reinforced the sense of prosperity and well being. I'm sure I'm not telling you anything you don't already know, but as generations grow and expand, we reach the point where growth is so slow that you have to look closely just to see what's going on. This is what has happened to our culture. Take away the microscope and the country seems to be chugging along, but at a closer look, many of the individual cogs in the wheel are being left behind."

"Isn't that the history of the developed world?" Dutch asked, looking at Johnny.

"Yes," Johnny responded, "but doesn't that create a larger necessity to help the unprepared, and ignored, with training and enthusiasm. Granted, it isn't the government's job to try and control everyone's destiny, but isn't that what Christ asks us to do? It is somewhere between rendering unto Caesar what is Caesars, and being our brother's keeper."

"Well isn't that why we have governmental social services?" John offered.

"And not just the federal government, but State and Local governments, not to mention the Red Cross, church disaster funding, and all the rest," Angie added.

"Those are all excellent points, and I agree with everything you've said, but..."

"I knew there'd be a but," Dutch interjected.

"But, Johnny repeated, when the person at the end of the line is confused, frustrated, under educated, or just can't figure it out, as Christians that is where we need to be standing. Is it a new idea; no? Has it been done before; yes? Is it time to take a closer look and see if we can help? I think so with all my heart. It is the subject of Christ's Sermon on the Mount, and to deny those wonderful ideas in the Bible's Book of Matthew is to deny our purpose here on earth."

"I told you he'd be a good preacher a long time ago, but you sent him off to build a youth camp," Dutch joshed.

Angie ordered a dish of lemon Gelato as the inspired

discussion they had just shared began to fuse into a battle plan.

☙

"Johnny, Ernie's gonna flip his lid," Brenda Sugg told Johnny Hendricks over the phone. "We've already got Dell and R.J. in the one dormitory and Ernie's got the other one piled with junk," she said. "We're getting too old to have little ones running around the house. I'm sure he'll be dead set against it."

"Have him call me when he comes in okay," Johnny said.

"Sure Johnny, you're pretty good at getting things done, but Ernie can be hard headed ya know, Bye now."

Later that evening Johnny and Eva were swinging on the front porch glider with Juanita in her lap. "Do you remember telling me that this was not your home and that you and Juan needed to make a fresh start?"

"I hope you haven't said anything to your mom," Eva said.

"No, your feelings are safe with me, but I have an idea that I would like you and Juan to consider."

"You mean right now?" She asked.

"If you want," Johnny said.

'Momento," she said, handing Juanita to Johnny and entering the house to find her brother.

"What's up, bro?" Juan asked squeezing in and making it a foursome on the glider.

"I have a possibility for the three of you that might help everybody, but it's only a possibility, not a commitment okay?"

"Sure Johnny, but you sound so secretive," Juan said.

The screen door opened and Angie walked out carrying a tray with three lemonades and a Sippy Cup for Juanita.

"It looks like the three of you are making plans, so I thought I would bring you some refreshments," she said setting the tray on the table. "I'll let you get back to business," she said returning inside.

Johnny told them about the Mission in Hancock and how it all came about. He told them about his friends Ernie and Brenda Sugg, and how they had been instrumental in making the mission project successful.

"I talked with Brenda this afternoon and told her about both of you and of course Juanita. I told her that it might be the perfect place for you guys to start over. I think we could refurbish that empty dormitory and make it livable for all three of you. Houghton is a nice little college town with lots of jobs and fun things to do, and maybe a chance for you both to get back into school." He paused and looked at both of them. "Now Ernie has the final say, and so far he hasn't called, but if it works out I think you should consider it."

The four rocked quietly except for the slurping sound of the empty Sippy Cup.

"We don't have any money," Eva said quietly.

"I wouldn't have mentioned it if there weren't good people to help you get started."

"It probably won't happen anyway. It never does," said Eva in her usual unpleasant manner.

"Hey Boyka," came a voice thundering into Johnny's phone a little later that evening.

"Ernie, I tink you jes woke up da whole neighborhood," Johnny said, answering the phone just after midnight.

"What's dis I hear you wantin to bring da whole world up to da U.P."

"Not da whole world Ernie, jes some good friends who need a new start," Johnny said.

"They been kind of down on their luck and I tink we could all help dem," Johnny said in his Yooper dialect.

There was ten seconds of silence.

"When you cumin up,"

"Next week."

"Bring em."

Johnny smiled as he climbed the stairs toward his bedroom.

ॐ

"Are you sure?" Del Souter asked.

"Here I'll let you talk to the boss," said Johnny handing Jenny the phone.

"Hi," she said. "How are things up in copper country?"

"Dare's two foota snow on Quincy Street and da lift bridge is closed, which as you know isn't too unusual for da Keweenaw in August."

"You know, Del I can finally understand you after only one year in Hancock," she laughed. "I think that might be some kind of a record."

"If you tink my talking is better, you should hear me play da banjo in Finnish."

"Here," she said passing back the phone to Johnny, "I'll let you talk to someone who thinks you're amusing."

"When do I have to move out of my office?" Del asked Johnny.

"Not anytime soon, although we should be back this coming week," he said. "I'll call you when we're on our way. How's that Irish colleen you spend most of your time with?"

"Fiona said to send along her love, and she's dying to

talk to Jenny to get caught up on what's happening with you guys."

"By the way, I'm bringing up some friends from New Mexico who need a little of your Kentucky wisdom, but I'll fill you in on that later. The Hendricks clan sends their love and we'll see you soon brother, Bye now."

On Friday an old pick-up truck with an over head camper pulled into Johnny's driveway. In the passenger compartment were two wizened faces trying to decide if they were in the right place. Victor approached the side door with Burt, his German shepherd at his side sniffing everything in sight.

The bearded man in bib overhauls with his formidable looking watch dog walking next to him, spotted Angie who was working in her flower garden in the back yard.

"Is dis where Johnny lives?"

"Yes it is," she said smiling, and I'm his mom Angie. Can I get that beautiful dog of yours a drink of water?" She asked, filling a bucket from the hose.

"It's nice to meet you Mrs. Hendricks. I'm Victor Wurtz, and dis here is Burt. I know Johnny from da Hospital," he said watching Burt stick his head in the over flowing bucket.

"Mr. Wurtz, you are a Yooper. I can tell, and I'm glad you dropped by. Go into the house and down the basement stairs and you'll find Johnny working out with his trainer."

Johnny was speed pedaling a stationary bike with sweat running down his forehead. Victor looked on in amusement.

"I'm tinkin you might wanna try anudder gear if you spect to get anywhere," Victor said, tickled with his own little joke.

"Victor, my friend, it's nice to see you. How did you find us?"

"Everybody knows where da famous Johnny Hendricks lives," he said. "Besides, me and Burt was in da neighborhood."

Johnny introduced Victor to Jenny and his trainer Stacy, who were happy to meet Victor in a curious sort of way.

Victor, never being one to beat around the bush asked, "When you leavin?"

"It looks like Monday morning; are you coming?"

"I tink I found a place for me and Burt to park our camper up dare, so, Ya I tink we'll go home too. I'll see you all sometime next week. Maybe we can talk to dis Bob Heikenin fella and straighten a few tings out, eh?"

"For sure Victor, I'm looking forward to spending some time with you. I've got some plans you might be interested in."

"Nice to meecha ladies," Victor said backing up the steps.

After he had gone, Johnny told his mom the Victor story, and she just smiled and shook her head.

∽∾

Word had gotten out that Johnny and Jenny were leaving on Monday, and the sanctuary at the Community Church was packed to capacity on Sunday morning. Johnny sat next to his dad behind the pulpit, and Angie, Jenny and the Ortiz family sat in the first pew. There was an air of celebration that everyone could feel. When the introit music was finished, there was anticipation in everyone's heart as Pastor John stood behind the pulpit. He looked out over the sea of friends and neighbors, and slowly began to clap his hands. The congregants, not quite sure of how to respond, began clapping their hands too. Pastor John clapped louder and faster and the expression of joy on his face was infectious.

"Praise God from whom all blessing flow," he shouted.

"Praise God from whom all blessing flow," the flock spontaneously shouted, and Pastor John laughed with pure love.

"Take comfort in the fact that in our darkest hour or our weakest moment, the love and joy we feel at this moment will always be there somewhere in our soul."

Pastor John waited for his parishioners to settle down.

"This morning a young man who was reared in this church family when it was only a neighborhood street meeting, is going to speak to us on a very important subject. He has wandered through the wilderness, been to the mountain and come out the other side reborn and refilled with the love and wisdom of the Holy Spirit. But first, let us all stand if we are able and sing together that wonderful old hymn, 'Softly and Tenderly Jesus is Calling', on page 27 in our hymnals"

The pianist began playing the opening strains and hundreds like a host of heavenly angels sang as one.

"See on the portals He's waiting and watching, watching for you and for me."

Half of the congregation sang, *"Come home,"* and the other half responded, *"Come home,"* and collectively harmonized, *ye who are weary come home, earnestly tenderly Jesus is calling, calling all sinners come home."*

The flock sat down emotionally spent, many with tears of joy in their eyes.

"It is not often that someone so close to you is touched by the Holy Spirit and raises the Banner of God to go forth and do His Holy works, but this morning we are blessed to be part of that movement. This morning, our son Johnny has such a story to tell. I pray that you will listen to him closely and respond in kind, Johnny?"

As Johnny approached the pulpit there was silence in

the sanctuary except for a small little girl's voice from the front row that shouted "Johnny," from her mother's lap, and pointed towards the front.

"Good Morning and I'm glad you're here," he said quietly. "I say that in all sincerity because I share a love of this place and your presence which goes back three generations. It hasn't always been in this facility or with the same people, but it has always been centered in the love of Christ," Johnny took a sip of water to clear his throat. "At this very moment across town, my grandfather is following in the footsteps of those Christians who left the Netherlands a generation before him, in hopes of finding the Jesus we read about in our Bibles today. The perfect yet fully human being who through His Father delivered the message to His followers and disciples passing it down to us here today. I bring you nothing that can't be found in the New Testament, only perhaps a new application of those blessed words. The word epiphany is not part of our casual daily conversations, but I mention it this morning because as the dictionary defines it, I have had a sudden striking understanding of where my future and purpose lies."

Johnny went on to tell the flock of his vision and the direction he was being led toward.

"I don't think the direction we are taking the Mission in Hancock is anything new or revolutionary, in fact, the New Testament lays it out pretty well; Love your brother; help your neighbor; follow the Ten Commandments; it's all pretty simple, and pretty general, and this is the problem. In the 21st century the computers and the smart phones have taken over our world. You hear the phrase, 'All things being equal'. It is a catch phrase to dehumanize the meek and the needy. I'm sure I'm not telling you anything you don't know or even anything we're likely to admit to. My point is simple.

We are hurting our brothers and sisters and they don't know how to defend themselves. History tells us that when we get too big for are britches we fall, and right now our pants as a nation are getting tighter, and if we are honest we're becoming concerned."

A slight murmur could be heard around the sanctuary, and more than a few heads began to nod in agreement.

"I'm sure that if we surveyed the congregation, many of you could name someone who is floundering and needs a hand up, so here's my plan. No, I'm not going to ask for more money," he said raising his hands in front of him.

The congregation began to snicker a little.

"The money this church has freely given has been used wisely and the work that the Hancock Youth Mission is doing today is a reflection on your generosity and grace. I intend to rally the faithful in our organization, roll up our sleeves, and find and help the most disenfranchised of our youth and give them a leg up to get back in the race to fulfill their destinies. This will come through job training, re-education and developing a greater sense of self worth. The Keweenaw Peninsula is a small area, but a perfect place to plant the seeds of self accomplishment and personal dignity. With your prayers and steadfastness, we can reclaim some of the youths who have faltered, and perhaps God willing, start a program that will grow in other areas."

The congregation uncharacteristically stood and gave Johnny an unexpected round of applause. John went forward and stood next to his son and said, "Let's all stand and turn to page 321 and sing 'Amazing Grace.'"As the congregation sang the endearing hymn, little Juanita clapped her hands with glee.

That night everyone helped pack the van with a special car seat for Juanita. Eva and Angie got to spend a little woman time together, as they made sandwiches and treats for the travelers. Angie who had spent most of her adult life in a world full of men hadn't realized how difficult it would be losing her only real female companion.

"I'll miss you mama," Eva said quietly as they bagged the food.

"You know, if I had a daughter and granddaughter, I wouldn't love them any more than I love you and Juanita," she said wrapping her arms around Eva. "We will all be here for you and Juan in what ever you do. God has something special in store for the three of you. I know it."

The next morning the temperature was in the seventies and the humidity was high as the six adults all hugged and said goodbye.

> *"Father keep your loving hands on this precious cargo as they travel north to do your will to complete their destiny. Amen,"* Dutch prayed.

CHAPTER 15

For the third time in less than a year, Johnny headed north from Grand Rapids towards the Upper Peninsula, this time in a brand new van, the love of his life, and three new explorers in search of their destiny. His last trip north was an odyssey of dreams and expectations based on the vision he had. It still surprised him how much he had changed and grown as a man in just seven months. It was tough to accept, but the dreamer was gone and the reality of the life he had chosen was at hand. The people in the Keweenaw who had listened to his vision, and bought into his plans were now part of the dream he had started and expected him to deliver. This wasn't some childhood fantasy. There were lives and futures at stake; three of them in the back of his new van. For the first time in a few weeks Johnny started feeling his old anxiety closing in on him. *Why had all of these people put their faith in me?* He thought. *What had convinced me that I could create this new project and pull it off? I've just spent the last six months proving I'm no Superman.*

Seeing the distress in his face, a hand slowly reached across from the passenger seat and patted his arm.

"How can I help?" Jenny said quietly trying not to wake up the Ortiz family in the back.

"I wish I knew," Johnny said. "I wish I knew how I got myself into this mess. I mean, nobody asked me to butt into their lives and turn everything upside down. If I had never had this crazy idea in the first place, everything would be just fine. No one would have great expectations; no one would be disappointed. I don't know what's happening to me Jenny but I get scared now. I just don't know," he said somberly.

"You know, your vision is good, and your plan is good. I think we can work with those two things, but once again it's your memory that's failing you Johnny Hendricks," she said pulling her hand away.

"What?" He asked.

"Once again you've forgotten who's in charge stupid," she said emphatically catching Johnny off guard.

Johnny's head snapped to the right looking into the eyes of the determined woman he loved.

"First of all, you haven't done anything that God hasn't given you after hitting you over the head to get your attention."

"But ..."

And second of all," she said beginning to raise her voice, "it's not your vision and it's not your plan. It's God's plan. You've got two friends running the Mission as well as you can, maybe even better, and you think you created them to be your assistants. Is any of this sinking into your thick skull Mr. Superman?"

"Well..."

And lastly, God didn't put me on this earth to fall in love with and chase after some egomaniac. You know God has better things to do."

Johnny scratched his head.

"If you think a good swift kick in the pants will put me in a more positive frame of mind then, first I agree with you; second I love you even more for explaining the facts for me; and third, now that you've woken up the whole van, maybe we should stop and get some breakfast. Okay Honey?"

After some bacon and eggs, Jenny climbed into the third row of seats and helped Juanita with her ABC's while Juan rode shotgun.

"Tell me about Ernie and Brenda Sugg?" Juan asked Johnny.

"I needed a favor, and a friend of mine suggested Ernie," Johnny started. "Ernie's an amazing man. He was the youngest of eight brothers and sisters who pretty much raised him after their mother died. He was a big hockey star at Michigan Tech. When the first Gulf War broke out he dropped out of college and joined up. Things didn't work out so well and he lost a leg. Walter Reed hospital gave him a new one, and he came back home and married Brenda. They couldn't have children so they decided to become foster parents and raised a bunch of kids who never would have had a chance if it hadn't been for them. Ernie's a carpenter and a handy man, and he made sure all of the kids that passed through their home had a good education or a trade they could fall back on. You should see their house on Christmas and New Year's Eve. The kids all come back to celebrate and there isn't even room to walk around."

"What was the favor?" Juan asked.

"A kid about your age got himself in some trouble and Ernie helped bail him out. You'll meet the kid and Ernie when we get there. In fact you'll all be living in the same house," Johnny said smiling.

They pulled into Marquette late in the afternoon and

Johnny and Jenny went into the Hospital to greet some old friends and show off his new legs. Juanita had had enough of the van and so Eva and Juan found a little city park near the hospital with lots of grass and some swings, and ran around for a while. An hour later they all met up, and after some fast food, the travelers once again headed north. The sun was still high in the sky as Johnny pulled up in front of the Sugg homestead near the top of the hill in Houghton.

Ernie and Brenda were sitting on the front steps and stood together as Johnny walked around the car.

"Who's da kid wid da new legs?" Ernie asked Jenny giving her a big hug.

"Just somebody we picked up below the bridge," she responded.

"Dis must be one of dem Trolls dat live under da bridge," he joked.

It was a long standing Yooper joke that people who lived below the Mighty Mack Bridge in the Lower Peninsula were called Trolls.

Juanita had her head buried in her mother's shoulder in fear of this big bearded man shouting at Uncle Johnny. Juan took Eva's arm and approached Ernie feeling a mix of fear and admiration.

"Gladameecha," Ernie said extending his big hand. "And dis is my wife Brenda," he added.

Brenda smiled at Juan and reached out taking Juanita off of Eva's shoulder.

"So this is our new love child," she said clutching the baby, and leading Eva up the front steps. "I think we'll get acquainted while the boys carry your things into your new home."

Eva had yet to say anything, shocked by the warmth of this welcoming woman. Brenda brought Eva and Juanita into the converted dormitory and showed her their new bedroom. After a quick tour of the apartment, Eva was once again shocked at how their fortune had changed and Brenda was surprised at how little the three vagabonds had brought with them.

The screen door slammed as Ernie led Juan carrying all the baggage into the tiny living room. When Brenda saw that Ernie had let Juan do all of the heavy lifting, she gave her husband the stink eye. Ernie immediately turned his back on her and led Juan into Eva and Juanita's bedroom. Thinking the toting was over; Juan sat down on Eva's bed.

"We've got one more trip to make," Ernie said rousting Juan up and leading him toward the boy's dormitory.

"R.J. dis is your new bunk mate. Juan dis is R.J." the two boys shook hands and Ernie left them to figure things out.

Johnny and Jenny waited on the front porch hoping to slip away to visit Helen and the Mission, but Brenda wouldn't let them leave without a quick bite to eat. It was impossible to turn down the hostess so it was ice tea and Finnish ginger snap cookies back on the steps. After a half hour of catching up, Johnny and Jenny left the Ortiz family looking like refugees standing between the Suggs. Johnny imagined that a lot of young foster kids had looked and felt the same way over the years. As they backed out of the driveway he leaned over and gave Jenny a passionate kiss on the lips.

"It's you and me against the world Baby," he said as they went down the big hill towards the blue Portage Lake Lift Bridge.

"You got it Rocky," she said playfully, glad to be home.

❧

When they drove by the Mission, there were only a few cars in front so they decided to drive down to Helen Aho's house. Helen, a sixty something widow and life long resident of the area was the first person Johnny had met back in October. In a matter of a few hours she had leased her late husband's defunct appliance store on Quincy Street to Johnny to build his new Mission, and also rented him a room in her home. They soon became great friends and confidants and the cornerstone of the future Hancock Youth Mission. Johnny's girlfriend Jenny was a college student at Michigan Tech and was rooming in a home a few doors down from Helen. The two women had met in church and had become friends.

"Toot your horn," Jenny said, as they pulled up in front of Helen's house, "so she'll know we're here. We don't want to scare her."

"Scare who," Helen said through the window coming from behind the van.

Johnny jumped out of the van and gave her a big hug. She was the closest thing to a Grandma he could remember and had missed her all the time he was in Grand Rapids.

Jenny ran around the van and asked, "How'd you know we were here?"

"You didn't expect a big mouth like Ernie Sugg to keep a secret did you?" Helen said laughing.

"I'll bet he's called everyone in town," Johnny said.

Just then, a car pulled up to the back bumper of the van and Paul and Del jumped out and the three men hugged and danced around like little kids. There were tears running down everyone's faces and nobody cared.

"You know," Johnny said wiping his nose, "I didn't realize how much I missed all of you until now."

They all crowded in and group hugged each other, and Johnny said,

> *"Father God, we are so grateful to be together and for another start."*

He started weeping again with tears of gratitude and joy, and never said another word.

Helen the sensible one said, "Maybe we all ought to go into the house. I have a reputation to uphold, you know."

"Lets all get back into the cars and head up to the Mission. I'm beginning to sense a party coming on," Del said.

When they all arrived back at the Mission, Ernie's truck was parked in front of the door.

"I told you he was a big mouth," Helen said.

Jenny smiled at Helen realizing that there was no other place in the whole world she would rather live than right down the street from Helen.

Cars started pulling up and parking on both sides of Quincy Street. The word was spreading like a California wild fire. Johnny was home. Twenty minutes later, the Hancock Youth Mission was packed. Outside on the street the crowd kept gathering trying to get a peek at Johnny with his new legs. Tom Burley, the Chief of Police pulled up to the Mission with his lights and siren blasting for the entire city to see and hear. It wasn't a warning; it was just his way of celebrating the return of the man he admired most in the whole city. Meanwhile, Johnny was inside telling anyone who would listen to go upstairs and take a seat. The street crowd was slowly sucked in through the front door and up the stairs to await their hero.

"I'm thinking you should run for office with a fan base

like this," Helen shouted to Johnny as they made their way up the steps.

"What office would that be?" Johnny shouted back.

"King of the world," she responded, but no one heard her over the ruckus.

"As he turned the corner on the second floor, a chant of "Johnny, Johnny," rolled from the mouths of the masses and they wouldn't be stilled. The public address system was quickly hooked up as Johnny made his way to the small stage, and everybody cheered as he grabbed the microphone.

"Hi," he said, and the pandemonium began again. Raising his hands to quiet the crowd, he said, "I missed you all more than you will ever know."

Several people, mostly women shouted, "We love you Johnny," and everybody in the building laughed, and then applauded the would-be admirers.

"I love you too," he said to quiet the crowd. "In fact I love you all, but more than that, I love the Lord who returned this broken man who was both emotionally and physically brought to his knees, and then raised him up, revived, and allowed him to come back home to fulfill his dream."

The throng began to settle down to hear what Johnny had to say.

"First of all I am able to get around on my own two feet, and in time with a lot more physical therapy I will regain full use of my lower body."

The celebration began again with shouts of "Praise God," their new mantra.

"Praise God, in deed," Johnny said, and the crowd quieted again. Secondly," he said somberly, we have yet to adequately deal with the death of our dear friend Bob Rogers, the young man from Toronto, Canada, who was just beginning to make his mark on the world with a bright mind and a fabulous sense of humor when he was taken from us. We will not let his passing go unobserved. This Mission as well as the friends he made here and his fellow Techies, will meet soon to plan a suitable memorial for this fine young man. As a community we can do nothing less."

Many in the crown had never seen Bob or knew much about him, but they were in full agreement with Johnny.

"And lastly," Johnny said, "for the work of Paul Rader, Del Souter, Howard Berg, and all the members of the Youth Mission Council we as a community owe you all a great debt of gratitude for working together in very troubling times, and sacrificing your personal lives and time to create and maintain this wonderful organization. Will you all please stand up and accept our thanks for your hard work."

Once again the citizens responded by acknowledging the team.

"There is much more to say, but now is not the time. I will be hard at work tomorrow morning with all the people I've just mentioned, not as the director of the Mission, but on a new project which you all will hear about soon. So, let's clear the streets and let our beautiful little city of Hancock get back to normal. Once again I thank you all for making this one of the most special nights in my life."

"Johnny, Johnny," resumed the chant as the revelers made their way down the steps and into a beautiful sun filled twilight embracing the Keweenaw. Johnny drove Helen and Jenny home, and when he pulled up in front of their house exhaustion set in.

"Ladies, if you want to go anywhere else tonight, I'm afraid you're going to have to find another chauffeur. I think it's going to take both of you to get me up the steps and into his bed."

CHAPTER 16

Del walked into his dormitory room and Juan and R.J. were lying on their beds talking. R.J. introduced Juan to Del and the two young men shook hands.

"So if you're not Mexicans, why do you have Mexican names like Juan and Juanita?" R.J. asked.

Del realized he had walked into the middle of a conversation and flopped down on his bunk hoping to learn more about his new room mate.

"Our parents were both born in Chihuahua, Mexico, a big city about a hundred miles south of the border at El Paso. They left their families and moved to Las Cruces, New Mexico for a chance to make more money. At that time there weren't as many restrictions between the two countries. Eva and I were born here and were immediately citizens, and then Juanita was also born here which made her a citizen," Juan explained.

"Is Eva your wife?" Del asked entering the conversation.

"No she is my sister," said Juan.

"Well then," R.J. asked, "where is her husband?"

"Eva has no husband. It's a long story which only Eva can tell, and so far she doesn't wish to tell it. She is raising

Juanita by herself, and I am just her proud brother trying to help in any way I can. I guess you must think it's all pretty complicated. I'm sure there must be young women with babies and no husbands here in Michigan."

"Juan I'm from Kentucky, that's another state, and I'm sure we have the same problem down there," Del said trying to seem worldly.

Juan smiled. "You guys know that if my name was John, in stead of Juan, you wouldn't be telling me where Kentucky is, and thinking that my beautiful little niece is a problem."

R.J. and Del looked at each other sheepishly.

"We probably would have asked you how you got such a great tan too," Del said.

All three of the boys laughed out loud, and the tension was broken.

"Okay," R.J. said, "let's start over. Tell us your story and we'll tell you ours, and then we'll open our own Keweenaw branch of young men looking for young ladies anonymous."

"I suppose the first seventeen years of my life were pretty much like yours," Juan said to his new room mates. I had a Mom, a Dad, and a sister. I was an average student, with not much to look forward to, just a teenager with brown skin looking for a way to get out. My skin was my passport to mediocrity. My folks had no money or ambition to do better or raise themselves up. You might think that their lives were unusual, but in the southwest border areas life was a dead end. Boys headed north and west, girls got married, had children and did what their mothers did, which was mostly living an unfulfilled existence. Our mother deserted our father and moved to Chicago; that's in Illinois by the way."

The two other boys smirked accepting their comeuppance.

"Eva, Juanita, and I tried to move in with her, but Mom wanted no part of us. There were too many mouths at the waterhole already, so we said good by and good riddance and moved east. We hitch-hiked our way up the Lake Michigan coast and ended up in Grand Rapids. We were hiding in a downtown vacant warehouse one night when Eva said she couldn't take it anymore. I woke up the next morning and she and Juanita were gone. I searched the downtown area in most of the places Latinos hung out, but they were gone. I begged and stole for a few days hoping that they would come back, but they were gone. I had nobody, no money and no place to go. I started looking for day work, but nobody would hire me because they thought I was illegal. Then one day the side door to the warehouse opened and Eva walked back into my life. She said she had found a place where Juanita would be looked after and fed while we planned our next move. I told her there were no next moves for people like us. Spending the next week looking for food or opportunities proved my assessment to be true. One night the side door opened up and a Mexican couple with a baby climbed the stairs looking for shelter. When Eva saw the baby she went crazy. The baby was a new born and had a horrible rattle down in her chest. It was obvious that without medical help she probably wouldn't make it. The next day Johnny's dad and mom found us, took us in, and Johnny told us that the Promised Land was here in Houghton, and here we are."

Del and R.J. sat quietly unable to say a word.

"Your turn," Juan nodded toward R.J.

"It's funny, but most of our early lives were the same. My parents were born here in the Keweenaw. My dad was a social outcast and my mother's life wasn't much better. At the age of sixteen she was driven from her home and into his arms. They ran a fishing business, had me and my little brother Jimmy and then turned on each other. Like you said, both of their lives were unfulfilled. I've spent the last few years stealing and selling car parts and trying to watch Jimmy. Long story short," he hunched his shoulder, "I got caught, went to jail, and if it hadn't have been for Johnny Hendricks, I'd still be there. You don't know it yet, but that man will change your life."

They both looked at Del.

"Ditto on the first part except I had really good folks, and I'm not really sure how or why I ended up sitting across from you two, but believe me I'm grateful that I am. Seeing Johnny come back up here in good health and a new vision to help everybody out makes me feel like I'm in the right place at the right time, and that's all I've gotta say on the subject."

The three young men sat quietly wondering what was next. A tap on the door announced that Juanita wanted to see where Uncle Juan was living.

☞

Helen let Johnny sleep in the next morning, and he wandered into the kitchen at the crack of 10:00A.M.

"Good Morning Helen," he said. "It's hard to believe I'm finally home."

"Well sit down for breakfast before you return the several hundred calls you've received so far this morning. I knew you were a big shot here in Hancock, but I had no idea we were going to need a receptionist here at home," she said serving up the pan cakes and bacon."

"Relax Helen, we'll take them one at a time and see what happens."

His first call was to Bertha Mittala, a member of the youth council, and his go to person when he needed organizational skills.

"Welcome home Johnny," she said. "We're all so happy you've made it back. I can hardly wait to give you a big hug."

"It's nice to hear your voice Bertha. What do you think about a Youth Council meeting tomorrow night at 7:00P.M. at the Mission? I know it's kind of short notice but I'm anxious to get back to work and see all my dear friends."

"I think that would be perfect Johnny. I've had three calls already this morning asking if I've talked to you. How are you feeling?"

"There are still a few joints that need a little more oil, but now that I'm home we can take care of that here."

It surprised Johnny how easy it was to call Hancock his home after living here such a short period of time before the accident.

"Well we've all been praying for you since the accident, and I'm looking forward to tomorrow night. If you don't mind, I'll take care of the coffee," she teased recalling his ineptitude in brewing their favorite drink.

"Okay we'll see you then," he said already looking for Bill Heikinen's number.

"Bill," he said, "Its Johnny."

"Welcome back stranger," he said. "I'm sorry I missed the grand entrance last night, but I heard you got the usual royal treatment."

"It's getting to be an embarrassment Bill."

"I'll have a little talk with our friend Ernie and tell him to tone it down a little. When can we get together?"

"Tomorrow night; Bertha has all the details. She'll call you with the specifics," Johnny said.

The morning was mild and Johnny decided to walk up to the Mission using his walking stick for support. Half way up the hill to Quincy Street he had to stop and catch his breath. Leaning on his cane he thought, *the last time I was here I didn't even notice this hill being here.*

"Good Morning my friend," he said to Paul Rader as he came through the entrance.

Paul came around his desk and hugged Johnny. "Here let me get you a chair," he said. "You know I noticed a little huffing and puffing as you climbed the stairs last night. I can only guess how much you've gone through since the accident, but starting now we're going to see that you take it easy."

"I've got to confess that at the moment I'm a very old twenty six year old, but I'm sure God's not finished with me yet," he joked.

"Finished with you, are you kidding? He hasn't even started using you. I guess you don't remember that less than a year ago this place was a derelict old junk heap, and now it's the crown jewel of Hancock. This is the biggest tourist attraction in the whole area. Your story has been written up in every newspaper in Michigan. Interviewers from all over the state, not to mention Wisconsin, have been waiting for you to come back just to meet you. You've replaced the Thimbleberry as the Keweenaw Peninsula's biggest enticement."

Johnny stared at Paul wondering if he was pulling his leg.

"How have you been Paul?" Johnny asked in all seriousness. "I know God dumped a heavy load on your shoulders, and you didn't even have time to figure what was going on or how it would affect your life. I prayed for you and Del every day hoping that this vision of mine and these plans of ours wouldn't overwhelm two of the neatest guys I've ever met. When Jenny came down to Mary Free Bed she told everyone what a blessing you two were to, not only the youth, but the whole community. We all said a prayer of thanks; I mean that sincerely. Now what can I do to help? Are you making enough money without your teaching job to keep your home and feed yourself?"

"I'm not sure if you know, or how much you know about the financing of our little Mission, but we've got a guardian angel who has taken over the business. Del and I get a check every Friday, and all of the expenses and paper work are covered in a timely manner. We get a statement every month from somebody somewhere telling us all the bills are paid, and to keep up the good work. It's amazing. Do you have any idea who's doing it?"

"I'm sure God has placed His mighty hand on our little Mission, as you call it, and is pleased with your efforts."

"I'm sure you know what you're doing, but I've got to tell you, it's not His name on the checks."

"I promise you it is Paul. You just don't recognize the signature."

Paul just smiled realizing the old Johnny was back and together they would be a blessing to the whole community.

"By the way, Bertha is setting up a meeting for the whole council tomorrow night at seven. See if you can get Del's brother and their Canadian friend Chuck to join us along with the other officers. I've got some ideas to run by the whole council to keep us moving forward.

CHAPTER 17

In spite of the summer season, there were many mornings in the Houghton/Hancock area when the temperatures in the early hours of the day were cool. The 50's and low 60's were not unusual with mist rising from Portage Lake.

"Shh," Eva said quietly to Juanita in the rocking chair on the front porch of the Sugg home. It didn't seem to matter what time she was put to bed, Juanita was awake and playing at first light. The screen door opened and R.J. came out on the porch with two cups of coffee and a juice box.

"Good Morning," he said handing Eva a cup. Juanita smiled and reached for the drink box.

"What do you say?" asked Eva.

"Thank you," said Juanita in perfect English.

"If we could teach her to say, "Thank you eh, she'd be a 'Latina Yooper,'" R.J. said, and they both laughed quietly hoping not to wake everybody up.

"What's on for today?" He asked.

"I've got to help Sherri open up the restaurant this morning. We have that big coffee and doughnut rush when we first open and she can use a second pair of hands for a couple of hours."

One of Ernie's many side lines is a small café called the

Hill Top Diner, a breakfast and burger joint he originally opened just to have a place for all of his foster kids to work and earn a little money. The place had become a Michigan Tech hangout where the students could get cheap eats and socialize. In the summertime when most of the students were away, the clientele were mostly working folks and regulars who just enjoyed the ambiance and the chatter.

R.J. and Eva had become close after they'd found out that their lives had run in similar paths. They were both take charge kind of individuals who were beginning to find themselves after former lives that neither of them were too proud of. They both owed their futures to Johnny Hendricks and his family, and were grateful for a chance to make good with a new start.

Del pushed open the screen and asked, "Y'all got room for another body out here."

"We've always got a place for our Kentucky roomie," R.J. said.

Juanita stretched her body toward Del wanting to be held by him. Del had charmed the little one by playing his 5 string banjo for her every afternoon. Juanita didn't realize that she was just a small part of an ever growing fan club. Del picked her up and bounced her around the front porch making them both happy.

"Dog," she said referring to the Salty Dog Blues, a song he played on his banjo.

"I jes cain't keep these ladies from digging my mountain music. It's a blessing and a curse. What's a country boy to do?" He said scratching his head with a false sense of humility.

"Some how I think you'll figure it out," said Eva with a smirk on her face.

"Brenda stuck her head out the door, and said, "I could use a little help in the kitchen."

As usual Ernie and Juan were the last two to drag themselves out of bed. It was becoming obvious that once again the professional foster parents had found a way to seamlessly bond together some more errant youths into a productive family.

⊙》

Johnny spent Monday afternoon with Kerttu Lehto and her son Kalle discussing his future plans for the Mission. Kerttu, a ninety-nine year old retired school teacher living outside of the old mining town of Boot Jack, had socked away a lot of money and was the chief financial benefactor of the Mission.

"Johnny you missed my birthday," she said in false disgust.

"And when was that?" He asked.

"Two weeks ago last Thursday," she replied as if everyone should know.

"Well," he stalled, "technically we didn't celebrate it on the actual date because I was a little busy, but now that I'm back we're going to throw you a party worthy of your young age. Can you forgive me and let me make it up to you?" He entreated.

"Johnny, you're such a sweet talker," she demurred. Of course you can."

Johnny made a mental note to mention Kerttu's birthday celebration at the Tuesday night council meeting. After all, if it wasn't for Kerttu, the Mission would probably be having bake sales on the sidewalk to make ends meet. It didn't make sense to ignore the gifts God was giving them. To Johnny it was actually a sign that the epiphany he had in his bedroom in Grand Rapids might actually be fulfilled, and if he and his team worked together nothing was impossible. Johnny had a smile on his face all the way back to Hancock.

His next stop was to take Jenny out for lunch at Kaleva's Restaurant. That was also a place he had missed while at Mary Free Bed Hospital, and when he and Jenny walked in the door they received a standing ovation from wait staff and customer's alike.

"Have you good folks lost your mind?" he asked enjoying every minute of the revelry. Linda Morgan, his new friend and associate Pastor of the Community Church on Quincy Street ran up to him and Jenny and threw her arms around both of them.

"Welcome home," she cried. "All of our prayers have been answered."

Linda had recently left her husband in Green Bay, Wisconsin and took her two young sons to follow her religious calling in Hancock. Johnny had managed to find her husband Brett a job in Houghton and helped reunite the family.

"There's two young men over by the window who want to give you guys a great big hug," she said leading them both to a table where Matt and Mark were laughing and waving their arms. When Johnny had first met them she jokingly introduced them as Frank and Jesse, the outlaws, but they soon lived up to their real names of the first two Gospel writers.

"Tell me what's going on at the church?" Johnny asked as Becky Wychoff served the new comers a couple of Cokes.

"Well, I gotta tell you," Linda said getting ready to explode, "our little church is on fire with the spirit. Since the summer season started we've had to add another Sunday morning service; not only because we're bringing in more locals, but when the tourists hear about the music on Sunday night they think it's a concert," she stopped in self realization, "in fact it is. It's a concert to celebrate God. Oh Johnny there's so much to tell you; so many good things. Oh" she stopped again. "You two love birds came here for lunch and I'm running my mouth and you two are starving."

"No, that's not true," Johnny and Jenny both protested, but Linda would hear none of it.

Becky who was patiently waiting to take their order said, "I've got a nice booth over here," pointing to a quiet corner.

"Perfect," said Linda. "We'll talk later," she said and shooed them away.

Once seated and away from the hoopla, Becky said. "Welcome back. I got the message from Bertha about the meeting tomorrow night. I'll be there. We all missed you Johnny, oh and the boss said lunch is on the house."

"I'll probably need a hand getting up there," he said, and the two ladies tried to ignore the corny joke.

"I think we can call the meeting to order," Howard Berg, the President of the Historical Society and Chairman of Youth Council said. There was a time when being the head of any committee gave him a feeling of self importance, but the events of the last ten months including his stay in the hospital with stress related health problems, and the hand of God turning his marriage and life around had him feeling nothing but love and gratitude this evening.

The people sitting around the table upstairs at the Mission were very dear to him now. There was of course

Johnny and Bob Heikinen, the President of the City Council; Tom Burley, the Chief of Police in Hancock; Father Walter representing the Houghton/Hancock Clergy Association, and Paul Rader, a junior high school teacher at Hancock Middle School who had taken a leave of absence to replace Johnny after the accident. Sitting next to Paul was Bertha Mittala, a mother, a community activist, and acting secretary for the group. Sitting quietly at the other end of the table were the teen representatives from the area. There was Lakeesha Johnson, a Michigan Tech sophomore from Detroit who was voted the youth leader. There was Rod Devlin, a local sophomore from Hancock High School. Next to him sat Becky Wychoff, a local high school graduate presently working as a waitress at Kaleva's Bakery, and Heather Burch, a pixieish youth from Traverse City who was re-entering Finlandia University in the fall after dropping out for a semester to try and find herself. Missing from the original group was Bob Rogers from Toronto, Canada, who was killed in the snow squall that had crippled Johnny. Two of Bob's buddies were invited to the meeting to help plan a memorial for him in September. They were Del Souter's brother J.D. Souter and Bob's best friend Chuck Atkins, also from Canada; both students were Techies.

"I think it would only be fitting and proper to have our dear friend and spiritual leader Johnny Hendricks to ask a blessing for our meeting tonight, Johnny."

Everyone nodded in agreement as Johnny stood with obvious difficulty and asked his fellow attendees to bow their heads.

> "*Father,* he said quietly, *seeing us all together tonight gives me profound joy, and also deep sadness. Part of my heart says thank you*

Lord for saving all of the lives of the people here tonight who rolled down that icy ravine to what seemed like certain death that fateful Saturday evening seven months ago. The other part of my heart continues to mourn the absence of our brother Bob, who was so full of joy and love that day. It is impossible to understand why he alone was taken from us, but we know where his heart was when he went home to You, and we can only thank You for the short moments we had with him. Father we promise to honor his memory by working even harder to make this Mission a place he would be proud to bring his friends to. Lift our hearts and open all of or minds to do your good works Lord, Amen."

Johnny held the back of his chair as he sat down, and his continuing physical struggle brought back thoughts of that horrible night.

"I think it might be helpful," Howard said, "if we turn over the discussion to Paul Rader to give us an update and an overall picture of the last seven months here at the Mission. I think a round of applause is in order for the fine job he has done, and the sacrifices he and Del have made to get this place up and running."

Howard started clapping his hands and everyone joined in as Paul stood up.

"First of all, I'd like to say that if it hadn't been for Johnny inviting me to help him collect some furniture in Grand Rapids last Christmas, I wouldn't be here tonight," Paul stood quietly for a moment. "I'm not sure I would be anywhere," he said almost to himself. "You know if there's any praise to be passed around I think that everybody in this room should take a bow. There isn't anyone here tonight who didn't stick their head in the door at one time or another, and ask how they might help or offer a little optimism when it was needed most. I lived here in Hancock for almost a year without making a friend until I took a day off from my teaching job, and came down here to help nail some boards. I don't know what brought me here, but I can tell you that up until that day I had never nailed a board in my life."

Everyone in the room laughed realizing that they could probably tell a similar story concerning the Mission and Johnny. In fact it took twenty minutes for those who wished to share a personal thought to relay a pleasant memory.

"I told Johnny yesterday morning that there's a guardian angel looking over this old building and it doesn't have anything to do with sweeping up all those big white heavenly feathers off the sidewalk every morning."

Once again everybody laughed.

"No, this blessing is something tangible. I don't know if you're all aware, but the bills are getting paid every month. Del and I are getting a check every Friday and it's more than enough to keep us going. Every month we're mailed a statement that gives us an itemized list of all the financial responsibilities that are being taken care of. Maybe it's none of my business, but I'm sort of curious what's going on."

Everyone looked at Johnny. Without standing up he said, "Paul and I kind of touched on this a little bit yesterday, but here's all I can share with you," Johnny said looking around the room. "Everybody here has demonstrated their devotion to this Mission by rolling up their sleeves and taking a hand's on approach to what needs to be done. But there are also people in this community who are unable to lend a hand, so to speak. Those good souls are able to help us out financially. Now, they don't want to be thanked or recognized as being cheerful givers. They get their reward from what they see us doing and the stories they read in the Mining Gazette. I can personally tell you that I have no idea who all of these generous folks are, but you have to remember that two churches in Grand Rapids footed the bills for a long time without even knowing where Hancock was. Once again all we can do is offer up our gifts and let the Lord do His mighty work. Can I get an Amen?" Johnny said feeling like a big time preacher.

Everyone said Amen.

"I think it's time to invite J.D. and Chuck up to the front, and open up the discussion for a memorial for Bob Rogers."

"My name is Chuck Atkins," a husky curly headed blond said approaching Johnny. Putting his hands in his back pockets he said, "Me and Bob have been mates since we started school in Kindergarten about fifteen years ago in Toronto. We didn't realize it at the time, but we were like two peas in a pod. We both liked sports, hockey mostly, and we both liked girls, and that kept us close friends through High School at Forest Hills High. Well, my folks were pretty well off and so were Bob's, so rather than hang around Toronto, we decided to apply to Michigan Tech in the U.P. They had a good Engineering program, a pretty good hockey team, and it was just far enough from Toronto that our folks wouldn't be dropping in at all hours," he said. "You know it comes to mind that our folks were probably thinking the same thing about our distance from them."

He smiled and tweaked his wispy mustache, and that brought a smile to everyone in the room including J.D. Souter.

"Anyway, both families got together and decided that we would probably be safer and better off together at the same school, so after a visit to the University and finding out it was only a comfortable two day trip by way of Sault Saint Marie, we both applied and were accepted together. School was easy for both of us, in spite of its reputation, and the student body was pretty nerdy, which pleased our folks. I've got to admit that Bob was more of a lady's man than I was, but that was okay because I started hitting the books and could actually see a future in what I was learning. Bob was kind of bored with school and probably would have transferred somewhere else if we hadn't dropped in at the Mission at that first open house. There were so many people on the ground floor that you couldn't move, so Bob and I went upstairs and sat in the third row right behind Rod Devlin. Johnny mentioned Rod from the stage and said that this kid, who's sitting across the table from me right now, had come with his track coach to see what they could do to help make a difference in the Keweenaw. Well, we stuck around most of the afternoon, and on the way home Bob told me that he had filled out his personal information on a clip board and couldn't wait to get back to this hallowed room." Chuck wiped his eyes and blew his nose. "You know," he said looking at Johnny, "before he went to that planning meeting; the day he died, he said that he was going to drop out of school at the end of the semester and join you and your Mission and try to make this world we live in a better place." There was not a sound in the room. "I took his body home that next week, and told his mom and dad and his brother and sister what he had said and what he planned to do, and we all cried together. Two hours later, after the tears, and the funny stories, Bob's mom Ruth said she was never more proud of her oldest son than she was at that moment. There was kind of a transformation in that living room. It was as if God came down and said that it was all right, and that Bob was at peace and that he was in a better place. You know, I went to visit the Rogers family everyday until I had to come back to school, and his mom always asked me to tell her about Johnny and the Mission. If we are going to have a memorial for Bob, I know the family and close friends and relative would like to come and be a part of it."

Chuck walked around the table, gave Johnny a brotherly hug and returned to his seat. J.D. stayed in his seat and said he had nothing to add other than that he would like to help as the go-between with the Mission and the University. The Committee sat silently not wanting to be the one to change the mood.

Lakeesha Johnson, the only African American most of the people in the room had ever met cleared her throat and said, "You know I remember that Saturday morning and afternoon, and If my memory serves me right, Bob was kind of a big tease. Now I don't want to say anything bad about our departed brother, but I didn't think he was ready for sainthood. My goodness, he teased us ladies unmercifully."

The three girls around the table began to smile. "I'll tell you what," said Heather, "I never had a big brother, but if I had one, he would be just like Bob."

"I'm sure he would consider that a great compliment," said Chuck having finally composed himself.

"It didn't seem to matter what anybody said, he always had something clever or funny to say," Becky added. "I don't know, he just seemed like a really neat guy."

"What about the second Saturday in September?" Johnny offered, refocusing the group. "The Labor Day weekend will have come and gone and everybody will be back in their regular routine. That gives us about a month to plan and we can contact Bob's family to see if they are available. What do you think?" Johnny asked the whole council.

"Let's do this," Bertha said. "Ask around to get a feeling for the date and what we could do, and call me. You've all got my number and I'll put together a package for all of you and then we can make a decision okay?"

"That would be terrific Bertha, does everyone agree?" Johnny asked.

It surprised Paul Rader how smoothly everything seemed to go when Johnny was in the mix. He thought *everything's possible when God's in charge.*

"Let's take a little break and then come back upstairs. I've had a new vision and it includes all of you," Johnny said. There was a low rumble as the committee went down stairs for some ice tea and some of Bertha's home made chocolate chip cookies.

Thirty minutes later the group sat in anticipation as Johnny whispered something to Howard and stood up.

CHAPTER 18

The pick-up with the camper on the back came out through the over grown rutted two track, and into the clearing. Burt was barking at all of the strange things in the yard; some covered with feathers, and some covered with rust. There didn't appear to be anybody home, but the new Dodge truck around the corner of the house gave him hope. Victor Wurtz had spent most of his life walking up and down old wooden steps in and around the Keweenaw Peninsula and the ones attached to this porch didn't seem to be too dilapidated. Burt sat at the bottom of the steps as Victor rapped on the door. He could hear the sound of the floorboards creaking as someone was shuffling across the kitchen. He hoped he hadn't wasted his time driving all the way out here.

"Good Morning," he said to the tiny old woman holding on to the screen door handle.

"What's yer bizness," the old woman said holding up her other hand to protect her eyes from the mid-morning light.

"My name is Vict…"

"I know who you are," she said, "and you've got no bizness here."

Her voice was the crack of a whip. Burt lifted his head to identify the source.

"I'm a friend of Johnny Hendricks and I want to help," the offended party said. "I know what most folks around here tink of me, but if you hear me out, I'll let you make da choice," he said standing back from the door.

"Halle!" She shouted into the house.

"I'm coming," said a voice that was used to taking commands. As his eyes focused on Victor, he said, "Victor Wurtz, as I live and breath. Everybody thought that you left town."

"More like escaped," said Kerttu Lehto not cutting the intruder any slack.

"Mrs. Lehto if you'll let me say what I got to say, den I'll be gone. Dis is about Johnny, not about me."

Kerttu was having so much fun disrespecting this alleged outlaw that she didn't want to let up.

"Sit in the rocker over there, and speak your piece," she said pointing across the porch. She and Halle brought out two chairs from the kitchen.

"Now I know you remember Ralph and Eileen Aitima from Baraga," Victor said.

Halle shook his head yes. Kerttu shook her head no.

"They were friends of dads. They were collectors." Halle said.

"And what did they collect?" Kerttu asked suspiciously.

"Metal scrap, and old cars and stuff, dey were friends of your husband and I was dare son, kinda."

"Kinda," she repeated with an eyebrow raised.

Victor started from the beginning and told her about the anti-Germans in the nineteen forties who burned down their farm and chased them away. He explained how Ralph and Eileen took him in and became his parents.

BRIAN K. HOLMES

"Dat's when I met yer husband Harold, Mrs. Lehto."

"Call me Kerttu," she said abruptly.

"Yes ma'am," he said.

"Ralph always said dat Harold was a genius. He used to come out to da farm and wander tru da whole acreage lookin fer somptin special. 'I'll know it when I find it,' he'd say and we'd jus let him roam around. More often den not, he'd find some little gizmo, and Ralph would tell him to keep it. Eileen always gave yer dad a couple Zucchinis to bring home. Ya he was a smart one dat guy."

"Tell us about Johnny," she said seriously; all the outrage gone.

"First I gotta tell you about R.J.," he said relaxing a little.

He left nothing out as he explained the whole saga to the Lehtos.

They were well aware of the problems that Kitty and Robert were going through and how R.J. took responsibility for his little brother Jimmy.

"I never took Jimmy, Kerttu. R.J. was jes tryin to help dat's all. I broke da law and I'm gonna make dat right, but right now I tink I can help Johnny." He pulled his chair closer as he explained what he had in mind. They spoke in generalities knowing that Johnny and the Youth Committee would make the final decision, but the three old timers all agreed that they wanted to help.

☙

The committee had not forgotten the tease Johnny had given some of them the night before. They were quite sure that he hadn't spent the last six months lying on his back without a thought of the future.

"I'm sure that when we hit our knees by the side of our

beds every night we start off with some sort of structured prayer or Mantra, but I wonder how many of us actually take the time to reflect on the reality of our lives, and sincerely ask for change or a way to be more useful to others. I would never wish on any of you the struggles I had this summer between God, and myself. A world of failure and incompletion can be more than a person living in perpetual pain can deal with. I'm ashamed to admit that more than once I cursed the heavens because of my plight. The realization was that although I tried to live a life in Christ, my inner self was hiding a dark secret that I was never able to acknowledge until the accident in February. It took a team of Physical Therapists, as well as a Psychiatrist and his staff to help me to realize that my heart was true, but the insidiousness of PTSD was stronger than I was, and without realizing it, I was victimizing myself. It wasn't until I was out of the hospital and rehabbing back at my folk's house that I had this vision. It came by way of a teenage boy, his sister and her baby. The three left their home in New Mexico in search of a new life, and ended up in Grand Rapids. It was there that the hand of God led them to the Hendricks family. We embraced these youngsters and helped them as much as we could. One day, Eva, the young mother of Juanita went to the Michigan Unemployment Office to try and find a job. In stead the two things she found were that the woman who took her application didn't care and neither did Eva. All she found out was that she wasn't qualified to do much of anything. And she was right."

Johnny tried to calm himself down. He wasn't sure if he was babbling or even making any sense. As a family who spent their whole lives helping others we collectively realized that there was a group we hadn't focused on. That group was the under educated or the under trained youth all around us who didn't realize that there was a more fruitful, satisfying life available if it was presented in a way that made sense to them. Are there a lot of them? I really don't know, but at a cursory glance I see enough to offer up this suggestion. First I will tell you what, and then I will tell you how we can maybe get involved."

Everybody present was taken aback. They finally had a chance to enjoy the presence of Johnny again. Wasn't their being together enough for now?

"I can see by your faces that you think I'm moving too fast, and maybe you're right. Please, I don't want to disrespect the fine work we've done together or to say that it isn't enough. I am not a dissatisfied over achiever who doesn't appreciate what we're doing here. Maybe my timing is bad and I haven't thought this through," Johnny said as he walked around the table with his head lowered and down the stairs.

Nobody stopped him. Nobody knew what to say.

"It looks like our brother is still fighting some demons," Howard said trying to figure out what just happened.

"I wonder if I might offer up a small prayer for our wounded brother whose heart continues to grow faster then we can keep up with."

> *"Lord, calm all our hearts and pull us together under the leadership of our brother Johnny. He has been through more than we can imagine, and more than anything he needs our love and support. We ask You to unify our hearts and hopes to understand the possibilities Johnny is offering. We continue to pray for his improving health so that we*

*can do your good work together what ever
that may be. Bless us all this night, Amen."*

Paul and Rod ran down the stairs in hopes of catching up with Johnny but Quincy Street was empty.

"Where do you think he went?" Rod asked.

"Jenny's," Paul said as they walked down the hill towards the lake.

"I'm sure it wasn't that bad," Jenny said rocking on her front porch swing next to a distraught Johnny feeling like he had destroyed everything they had all worked so hard for.

"You didn't see the look on all of their faces. I must have sounded like a crazy man running my mouth in the face of all they had accomplished. This is a nightmare, and I'm afraid I won't wake up."

Jenny didn't know whether to tear into him again, or comfort him until he realized he was over reacting. She knew it was a possibility that he might run into the same fears and insecurities he fought at Mary Free Bed, but sooner or later he had to start putting one foot in front of the other and walk his way out of this funk he had created.

"I'm not sure that I'm the right person to be telling you this," she said, but here's my two cents worth. Johnny you have been out of sorts for so long that you don't remember what sorts are. You have been in pain and despair since last February. Seven months is a long time to go through what you have gone through, especially when your only enemy is you. There are no pats on the back or atta boys which will give you the confidence or comfort you had before the accident. I love you. Everyone in that room tonight loves you. The only one who doesn't love you is you."

"Amen," said a voice from the front yard.

"Who's there," Johnny said sitting up erectly.

"The ex school teacher whose soul you saved on the road to Grand Rapids last Christmas, and the teenager who thinks you walk on water."

"I'm so sorry guys; I really blew it tonight," said Johnny lowering his head in shame. "I'm so embarrassed for the things I said tonight. I wish I could have a do over."

"You'll get a do over as many times as it takes to get this plan of yours right," said a voice walking up behind Paul and Rod.

"Is that you Howard?" Johnny asked.

"It's me and everybody who loves you from our meeting who need a little more information on your new vision."

"If it's as good as the last one we can hardly wait for our new marching orders," said Lakeesha, standing between Heather and Becky.

"You're all crazy," said Johnny blowing his nose into a Kleenex Jenny had handed him.

"Well come up on the porch and let's talk about it," Johnny said feeling a little bit better about the evening.

Rather than talk about a new vision, the group just wanted to tell stories about the old Johnny and how despite a few differences of opinion, they had all worked together to help create the most beautiful thing they had ever done in their lives. The younger members had never heard the stories about the Johnny and Howard rivalry, and none of them could believe that they weren't always best friends. Bob Heikinen told the story about the night that R.J.'s brother Jimmy disappeared and Sheriff Burley broke up the Council meeting just before they were about to decide on the Mission.

"Yes sir," Tom said. "That was one for the books."

"That was the first time we all got a chance to meet the whole Hendricks family," mused Bertha.

To Johnny that first month he was up here seemed like ancient history, and the few months that followed had, turned people of like minds into true friends; his friends.

"So what do we do know?" Paul asked to no one in particular.

"We could sell the Mission and have a big party," Chuck joked to lighten the mood.

"You know, that was something Bob would have said," noted Becky.

"Maybe it's just a Canadian thing," said Heather, and they all laughed.

"I think that little quip just voted you into the inner circle to take Bob's place as our Canadian representative. All in favor say aye," Johnny said.

The front porch masses hollered "aye".

"The next order of business is electing our inter-state representative from the great state of Kentucky, the Honorable John David Souter. All in favor say Aye as well," Johnny continued.

"Aye as well," the smart aleck committee responded.

"I have a feeling we're not going to get much accomplished," Johnny said, "But we'll have a great time doing it."

"Amen," shouted the assembly.

CHAPTER 19

A week later R.J. walked into the Hill Top Dinner and sat at the counter.

"One coffee black please," he said to Eva who was folding silverware into napkins.

"Well this is a welcome surprise," Eva said, setting the cup in front of R.J. "Aren't you and Del working this morning. It's been a week since I've seen you. I thought maybe you moved out. I wouldn't blame you with my brother for a bunk mate."

"No, Del has been showing Juan the ropes, as they say in New Mexico," R.J. said with a smirk.

"And you?" She asked putting her elbows on the counter and looking into R.J.'s eyes.

"I'm working on a special project that Ernie's involved with. I'm not too sure what it's all about, but so far we're just plotting out property lines, and cleaning up junk and stuff like that."

"Here in Houghton?" She asked.

"No, south of town a little ways," He answered. "I'll let you know what's going on when I find out, okay."

"Sure R.J.," she paused, "By the way Juanita's always

asking about you, so if you want to, you can stop by and say hello once in a while."

"I'll do that," he said as he headed for the door.

As he backed out of the parking spot and headed for Baraga, he wasn't sure why he stopped at the Hill Top for coffee, but the more he thought about it he knew he was going to spend some time with Eva and Juanita. After all, she did invite him.

Ernie was already unloading his truck at the old Victor Wurtz Junk Yard at the Baraga Plaines Road job site. When R.J. arrived, they would start loading up the big dumpster with all of the junk that Victor had left behind and see if they could get that old bulldozer fired up. It really was a junk yard, but there were still some useful pieces of equipment lying around which he could use to help create a building site. He wasn't sure who owned the property, or what they were going to do, but if Victor and old Kerttu were behind the project, who was Ernie Sugg to stand in the way of progress. After all those two old timers were around here before there was much of anything. Besides, he didn't want to be on the wrong side of a Finn and a German working together.

R.J. pulled into the parking lot, grabbed his tool box and a five gallon can of fuel for the Bulldozer and met Ernie around behind the shed.

"I thought you were going to stop and get us a coffee at the Hill Top Café," said Ernie.

"Well I stopped, but I forgot to bring you one," R.J. said.

"You forgot," Ernie said indignantly.

"I guess I had other things on my mind," R.J. stumbled.

"Did those other things include a pretty waitress who probably served you a cup?" Ernie was starting to figure it out.

"Well, I won't forget the next time," R.J. said feebly.

"Next time! What makes you think there's gonna be a next time. Tomorrow morning I'm stopping with you and we'll both have a coffee, and you're buying, okay?"

"Yer da boss," R.J. said dragging the fuel can up on the front of the dozer.

Two hours later under a clear blue sky a huge belch of black smoke exploded out of the exhaust pipe befouling all of the air around the two smiling men.

"It just needed a little love," Ernie said as R.J. continued to jam his foot on the gas pedal as the mechanical leviathan continued to try and resist the inevitable. While R.J. worked the four different positions of the lift blade, Ernie walked around the beast injecting grease into as many fittings as he could find. Slowly with the dozer in forward gear, the yellow brute moved forward dropping clots of clay from the tracks. Like a Wild West bronco buster R.J. gave her the gas as he mowed down every tree and bush in his path.

There are some folks who are meant to sit in an office and stare out the window, but this is the life for me, he thought as he waved his hat at Ernie smiling back at him. His instructions were to level the top ten acres by the road, and drag all of the big stumps off to the side. He couldn't believe he was getting paid for playing with this big toy. On his third time around the perimeter, he noticed Victor Wurtz's camper truck in the parking lot.

"I wondered when you'd show up," R.J. said, unsure of whether he should shake his hand or not.

"Like a bad penny," Victor said grabbing R.J. in a bear hug and lifting the young man in the air.

Despite the mixed feeling about the reunion, R.J. truly was happy to see his old friend again. R.J. looked over at

Ernie uncertain what was going on or what the boss was thinking.

"I'm gonna go get that cup of coffee you owe me," he said. "I'll be back in an hour." With that he jumped in his truck and drove out through the gate.

Victor held R.J. at arms length, and then hugged him again.

"Come on; let's go sit in da shade. We got some tings we gotta talk about." The two men went and sat under a shade tree on two big rocks.

"You go first," R.J. said.

"Well first, I gotta say yer workin on yer own property. When I cut outa here on da run I didn't have nobody but me and Burt. I knew I could explain away hidin yer brudder up here at the Yard, but dare was no way I could explain away yer stealin and me sellin all dem car parts. I was for sure a crook, but you were only eighteen and widout me around I taut dat da law might go easy on you. It probably wasn't a good idea, but it was the only one I had. I'm sorry I ever got any of you boys in dat mess, but dat's all behind us. When me and Burt left here, we stopped in Marquette and did some tradin wid my partners in da thievin bizness. When da Feds raided dis place dare was nuttin to link you or me to anyting. Anyway, I went down to Grand Rapids to find a brudder I didn't know I had. It was just one a doze crazy tings. Long story short, I gotta janitor's job at Mary Free Bed Hospital, and one night I was dustin da floors and I went into Johnny Hendricks's room. I saw da name on da door and wondered if dis might be da same guy from here ya know. I know it's crazy, but we got to be friends. He got healthy and said he had this vision and was coming home. He asked if I wanted to come home too. R.J. I ain't got no place to go. Dis was all I had," he said.

R.J. sat on his rock just picking a scab, wondering what was going on. Nobody's gonna believe this he thought.

"So I say to myself, maybe dare's some way I can make tings right. So I drove up here a couple a weeks ago, and I remembered Johnny sayin dat he talked to Kerttu last winter, and she was helping da Mission. So, last week I drove down to Boot Jack and talked to Kerttu and Halle and..."

"Now wait a minute, who are they?" R.J. asked.

"Oh, oh, maybe you better forget dem names, I tink I misspoke."

"This is the most confusing story I've ever heard," R.J. said walking towards the bulldozer.

"Tell Ernie I'll call him," Victor yelled as Johnny fired up the bulldozer.

An hour later Ernie pulled into the lot with a bag full of burgers and fries. They sat in the cab of Ernie's truck and chowed down with the air conditioner on, and both were quiet for a while.

"What did you and your buddy have to talk about?" Ernie said jamming a fist full of French fries in his mouth.

"What makes you think he's my buddy?"

"Cause he told me the whole story."

"When was that?" R.J. asked.

"About a week ago," he said. Ernie finished his pop and burped so loud that R.J. had to role the windows down to and let out the foul air.

"Do you mind letting me in on what's going on?" R.J. asked.

"Can you keep a secret?" Ernie asked.

"I think so," R.J. answered.

"This is not some school room secret. This is a secret that can hurt people and ruin lives. It's that important."

"You have my word Ernie. I kept Victor a secret and this will be the same thing."

"This property we're sitting on belongs to you and we're going to build a training center on it"

"This is Victor's property," R.J. said adamantly.

"He gave it to you. I saw the paperwork. Didn't he tell you?"

"He mentioned something crazy, but I didn't believe him."

"He's a changed man R.J. The crook you knew is gone. I think he had one of those come to Jesus meetings with Johnny in Grand Rapids and ever since he's been kind of on our team. Do you get it?"

"How come you're tearing up my property?" R.J. asked with a false indignity.

"Now don't get cocky boy or I'll run you over with your own bulldozer."

R.J. just stared out the windshield unable to fathom what he had just heard.

"And close that side window, your letting out all the cool air."

Ernie and R.J. knocked off early and went their separate ways. R.J. rushed home, took a shower, put on his best jeans and a clean shirt and knocked on Eva's door.

"Who is it?" came a little voice at the bottom of the door.

"It's R.J." he answered hearing the sound of little feet running away.

"I didn't think you'd come visiting this fast," Eva said opening the door with a smile.

"Well I was in the neighborhood," he said looking back down the hallway where he and his two bunk buddies slept.

"Come on in," she said standing back.

"I've got a better idea," R.J. said. Why don't I come back in half an hour and the three of us can go out for ice cream."

"That would be great," she said. "I'll get some clean clothes on Juanita."

R.J. drove up to Calumet where a new café with an ice cream bar held Juanita's full attention as she stood on her tip toes trying to see into the big bins of the frosty goodness.

"Chocolate please," the little one said smiling at R.J.

"Miss," said the young boy behind the counter looking at Eva.

"You choose," she said looking at R.J.

"Tommy, give us both a couple of scoops of that strawberry vanilla please."

While Tommy was dipping the cones, R.J. told Eva that the best strawberries in the area came from Chassell, just south of Houghton. The three sat on a bench on the shady side of 5th Street licking their cones and watching all of the tourists enter the Copper World Gift Shop looking for unique gifts made of native copper. Eva took a damp wash cloth out of her purse and cleaned her daughter's hands and face.

"Wanna see one of the Keweenaw's most beautiful sunsets?" he asked.

"We'd love to," Eva said taking Juanita's hand and R.J.'s arm as they walked back to the car.

Despite the unremarkable name for such a beautiful a spot, people around the area sort of ignored it and took pleasure in the combined rocky sandy beach of Water Works Park. There were always agate hunters, bent over the rocky sands looking for the rather common stone, which when polished usually became a treasure or a fine ring. Juanita took off her sandals and waded through the warm water holding hands with R.J. and Eva. R.J. had brought a blanket from the back of his truck and as the sun started dropping in the western sky. The three of them found a grassy spot on the cliff to lay their blanket and joined the crowd in the ageless tradition of watching the sun disappear into Lake Superior. Everyone cheered, and Juanita clapped her hands as the temperature cooled and folks started walking toward their cars. R.J. could never remember being happier as Eva placed Juanita in her car seat, slid into the front seat, leaned over and gave R.J. a kiss on the cheek and said thank you.

CHAPTER 20

The next day Bob Heikinen called Johnny early in the morning and said "Kaleva's,10:30 this morning and bring an appetite," and hung up.

Johnny still wasn't sure what was going on when he walked in the front door of the restaurant and searched for his mentor and friend. He spotted Becky taking a food order and gave her a wave.

Bob hailed Johnny from a booth by the window. The two men embraced in the usual manly way and slid into the booth.

"How are you this morning," Bob asked, "and I'm as serious as can be. Our meeting last night opened my eyes to some things I wasn't aware of."

"Good Morning guys," Becky greeted dealing out he menus. "Breakfast, lunch, or beat it." She offered with a smug look on her face.

"Wow," said Johnny, "dis town is getting to be a tough place, eh," he said with a wink. "You's guys was never dis way back in da old neighborhood."

"Maybe a couple of coffees and a few minutes please," Bob said.

"Coming right up gentlemen," she said.

"What was that all about?" Johnny asked Bob.

"That's why we're here Johnny. A lot of people are a little confused about the Johnny who came back to us."

"Let me…"

"No Johnny let me. I'm the one who must apologize. I'm the one who let you down, and I'm the one who is going to straighten it out."

"But…"

"Come on, let's get out of here," Bob said as Becky approached with the coffee.

"I'll keep em warm," she said holding up the drinks as the two men exited the café.

Bob drove up the hill to the Lakeside Cemetery and turned the car off. Both men looked out at the sea of graves without speaking.

"I've got a brother here, and Rod Devlin's got a dad here. I'm not sure why, but this place gives me a lot of peace. Now I want to continue talking, and I want you to continue listening."

Johnny nodded wondering what was coming next.

"You know the first time I met you I was sitting there trying to figure out how I could let Helen down easy. If I said no to your plan she would lose the possibility of selling that derelict building. I knew she needed the money and maybe there was a possibility that you might be for real and perhaps you could do something to help our historic district. And then you told me your story and my whole opinion of you changed. In a twenty minute period you made me a believer. Not only that, but I really liked you, and believe me that doesn't happen very often."

Johnny looked over at Bob and recalled that cold afternoon in October when his whole future was on the line. All he could think of was calling his parents and telling them that he had failed.

"You know I remember that afternoon too," Johnny said, "and other than the thought of failing, I remembered that I really liked you too. You reminded me of my dad and Dutch. While you were talking I was praying that God would change your mind and hopefully we could work together. I new I wasn't the man for the job, but I thought I could do it with an ally like you."

The two men sat quietly again. There were people around the cemetery oblivious to the two men in the car. Some employees of the county were cutting grass and trimming around the grave stones, and some placing flowers and wreaths.

"Johnny, when they called me and told me that you and Rod were on that helicopter headed for Marquette Hospital, I prayed harder than I ever have in my whole life that you would come back to us," his voice lingered, "because I couldn't imagine a life without you in it. When we received that wonderful call saying you were banged up, but that you would survive, I was grateful to God like never before. Seeing you in the wheel chair was tough to accept, but you had pulled off so many miracles in the few month you were here that it seemed inevitable that you would bounce back and be the same old Johnny that we all knew and counted on."

"That Johnny died in the accident on the coast road," he said morosely, "and the one they delivered to Grand Rapids for rehabilitation on his legs was the person I was to become. You wouldn't have recognized me either. While I was trying to be the old Johnny, a secret I had kept inside of me for nine years raised its ugly head and almost consumed me," Johnny said staring straight ahead. "It was a couple of months before

I even knew I had changed. In the meantime everyone around me had to suffer through my anger and self pity."

"That's my point Johnny," Bob butted in. "Those of us who were on your team thought that if Mary Free Bed fixed your legs, they would ship you home to us as good as new and we could start again. I was the one who should have kept tabs on what was happening to you and helped people to prepare for this victim of a horrific accident, and the complication of the PTSD that took over your brain. When you came home to us, none of us were prepared for what God offered us."

"And what was that?" Johnny asked.

"A beloved friend who had been given new marching orders from God and a body not yet ready to fulfill them," Bob said.

Johnny watched a white flower truck from a florist in Hancock stop at the end of their row, and consulted a clip board to find the final resting place of some ones dearly departed.

"So what now?" Johnny asked.

"Let's go down to one of those fast food joints in Houghton and get a couple of those indigestion burgers and find a quiet place on the Hancock side of the Lake and you can tell me the first thing you remember when you woke up in a bed in Marquette."

CHAPTER 21

The Youth Committee met the following Thursday evening at the Mission to plan the memorial for Bob Rogers. Del's brother J.D. and the rest of the men living in their student housing were all present as well as the rest of the Committee. It had been planned that Bob's family in Toronto would be hooked up on a conference line so that their input could be used for the Memorial.

"Hello," Rob Rogers said.

"Is this the Rogers family?" Johnny asked.

"Yes and I'm Rob Rogers, Bob's dad, along with my wife Ruth, Bob's younger brother George, and sister Grace. How are you all doing this evening?" Rob asked.

"We're fine Rob. I'd like to introduce our Committee to your family before we get started."

"Thank you Johnny that would be great."

The last one introduced was Chuck Atkins.

"Mr. Rogers, we've all talked it over and if you are having a problem understanding our American, we can switch to Canadian."

Both ends of the phone line were silent for a second, and then everyone burst into laughter. Chuck had broken the ice for a lot of nervous people and gracious conviviality ensued.

Chuck took over the conversation with nods from members in Hancock, and Ruth Rogers offered their suggestions with both sides of the border agreeing wholeheartedly. Johnny took over for the summation.

"I think we've got a pretty good grip on the situation," Johnny said, "but let's make sure we've got it right. We will expect to meet your family on Friday morning, the 8th of September at 9:30 in front of the Mission. We will have breakfast together and then Chuck, Paul, and I will give your family a tour of the Houghton/Hancock area. At 6 P.M. that evening we'll meet upstairs with anyone who would like to attend for a dinner of Finnish/American delicacies, including Pasty's from Toni's internationally famous bakery, followed by an open house memorial, to give Bob's friends a chance to share their love. Bertha," he said to his go-to woman, "we'll need a sign-up sheet for the meal and the open house. Get with me later for the cost of the meal. The open house will be free."

"Excuse me Johnny," Rob interrupted. "That is very generous of you, but the Rogers family will pick up the entire cost of the meal on Friday night, including all of the help you will need to make it a glorious evening. We would consider it a privilege to treat Bob's friends and share their love."

The Committee could hear Ruth sobbing in the back ground, with Grace trying to comfort her.

"I'm sorry, I…" Johnny said.

"We want to see where Bobby died," sniffled his mom.

"I'm sorry Johnny…" a bereft father interrupted embarrassed and anguished at the same time.

Both ends of the phone connection were weeping together.

"Ruth," Johnny said," You have my word that we will

all lay a wreath on that hallowed ground on the shores of Lake Superior and offer a prayer in his memory. I assure you that his memory will be the center of everything we do that weekend."

"Thank you Johnny," she whispered.

Clearing the huskiness from his voice, Johnny prayed,

> *"Dear God in the midst of genuine fellowship, the longing innocence of a mother cries out for her lost child. Father we know that he rests with You, fully restored, free of pain. We know that in the fullness of time we all will share that love together, Amen."*

There was silence mingled with sniffling as all who had experienced the precious memory of a loved one gone. Words were not enough to fill the air.

"Rob, Ruth, George, Grace, All of us here in this room have a better understanding of where you're wonderful son got his humanity. We will talk again in the next few days, and finalize this special memorial. We love you."

"I need a soda," Johnny said walking toward the pop machine followed by an older wiser committee.

An hour later:

"Becky, you and Rod are in charge of the local menu for the breakfast on Friday. Anybody want to get involved, see them. Lakeesha, I'm going to give you the ceremony as will as the finger foods down stairs after the memorial; get with me and Bertha for details. If there are no other pertinent questions on the subject," Johnny stopped for a second and looked around. "Then the next topic I would like to talk about is me."

Everyone in the room sat up a little straighter in their chairs.

"First I'm going to give you a little synopsis about what's been happening since I last saw some of you tumbling around in my old van last February. As you can see outside the door, the old van has been retired and replaced by one that will hold a few more of us. Lakeesha, as much as you and Paul liked riding way in the back, because of your lofty committee positions, you have been relegated to riding right behind the driver."

The committee began to loosen up a little, sensing Johnny was in one of his lighter moods.

"On a more serious not, I need to explain a few things about my stay in Grand Rapids." Johnny went on to explain the physical therapy he received at Mary Free Bed Hospital and his need for continuing his daily exercise to help with his recovery.

"Now I'm going to tell you about something even I didn't realize until after the accident." He explained his PTSD condition as completely and honestly as he could. "You saw a little of it last Thursday night when I couldn't deal with the moment and had to escape. I am currently working with a counselor and taking medication to work my way through this situation. I also offer you this thought. There are more people suffering from the effects of PTSD caused by accidents and abusive behavior than by war time circumstances." Johnny looked around the room. "If there is anyone here, or maybe someone you know who is suffering from a hidden anxiety or even something that doesn't seem right, come and see me and we'll find someone to listen. Most of the old Johnny is back. The brand new Johnny with a screw loose is standing before you and so very glad to be alive and back in the Lord's service. Now, if you don't go down stairs right now and eat all of Bertha's goodies she'll probably blame me. Go and enjoy and thanks for listening to me."

Bob Heikinen walked around the table and gave Johnny a hug.

"I love you," he said putting his arm around the new Johnny's shoulder and escorted him down the stairs.

There was renewed buoyancy around the soft drink bar as Bertha and Heather set out the trays of pizza snacks and pop corn. No one felt the urge to run out the door. Johnny had brought it all back together, and everyone was grateful.

"I'm not very good, but I bet I can beat anyone in the room at ping-pong," Johnny challenged.

"Let's make it double's," Chuck said, "Me and Johnny against the world." The mood was a dream that Johnny longed for during those depressing months in Grand Rapids. Praise God from whom all blessing flow.

☙

The following Monday morning, Paul and Johnny were sitting in the kitchen of the Mission discussing the guest list for Bob Roger's Memorial. Although most of Hancock's citizens were aware of the ceremony because of the newspaper coverage, it was difficult to tell who would deem it important enough to take a Saturday off to attend. The Michigan Tech Huskies had a home football game against Northern Michigan later that afternoon. It was a big rivalry game, and unusual to be played so early in the season.

"Good Morning," said Del approaching from the hallway. "It's always a pleasure seeing my two superiors engaged in planning the schedule for the whole universe, or maybe something less than that."

"What's up?" Paul asked.

"Ernie said he needs both of your expertise on something to do with the Mission. He said it wouldn't take a minute and you could ride with me, and best of all he'll buy lunch."

"I hope he doesn't think he can buy our time for a burger and fries at his own little café," Paul said jokingly.

"I think we can finish this later Paul, let's go see what Ernie's up to," said Johnny.

"Where are we going?" Johnny asked as Del drove south towards Chassell.

"We're working on a job sight down here. That's all I can tell you." Del said.

"I'm thinking steak," said Johnny.

"I'm thinking steak and lobster," responded Paul.

Del took a right on State Hi-way 38 in Baraga and soon drove passed the Ojibwa Casino.

"There goes our steak," Paul said as they passed the crowded parking lot at the gambler's paradise.

On the Plains road Del took a left and pulled into an empty field with two rows of cars, butting up against a big white tent.

"Do you want to tell us now?" Paul said leaning forward to look into Del's eyes.

"Nope," Del said slamming the door and running into the tent.

"Would it be redundant to say that something's going on?" Johnny asked.

"Nope," Paul said as they entered the tent.

"SURPRISE," everybody yelled as the two men stood waiting for an explanation.

"Dey don't seem to be too surprised," cackled Victor.

"No dey don't," said Kerttu slapping Victor on the back.

"Johnny, I'm da one who's caused dis ruckus, so sit down and I'll do da talking," said Victor.

All of the envitees including Paul and Johnny sat down on folding chairs while cold drinks were passed out from a cooler.

"If you don't know my story in da Keweenaw, go down to da newspaper, or da jail, del both have it on file," Victor said by way of an opening. "Da new story is what I'm telling today. As mosta you know, Johnny's da right hand of God up here and who ever he touches, well it turns out pretty good. He don't tink nobody knows his bisness, but we do. Raise yer hand if you tink I'm right."

Everybody raised their hands.

"I already talked too much. Here it is Johnny. Dis property wer sittin on belongs to R.J. Hackala, one of da finest young men I know. Now here's da plan. Ah, you tell em Mr. Heikenin. I can't talk no more," and Victor sat down to a huge round of applause. The first one he ever got in his whole life. He just sat there running his fingers through his beard like it was a mistake.

"Johnny, a week or so ago you spoke to a group of your biggest supporters," Bob said. I know that it didn't get the response you'd hoped for, but like Lincoln's Gettysburg Address, you said all of the things that needed to be said to fulfill the promise to God when we started this Mission. We all left that meeting feeling that there must be more. Once again the Hand of God was raised, not by a band of angels, but by a simple kindly man who ran a junk yard; who heard your heart down in Grand Rapids and set the ball rolling. All the people sitting around you now have in some way committed who they are or what they have to building a community training center on this property. This will include the buses to bring these young people here and back as well as the many citizens' with unique skills to help train the next generation. We are not here to compete with the school systems, only to augment what they are doing to give everybody a chance to try something that's not available now. The heart of our program will always be the Youth Mission on Quincy Street, but thanks to your vision Johnny we now have new marching orders. Can I hear an amen?" Bob shouted.

"Amen," rang from every voice as they raised their soda cans on high.

All eyes were on Johnny as he struggled to stand. "I think I have a vague idea of what's going on here," he said looking at each individual around the table, "and I assume that the big fellow bending over the ice chest would like to tell us all what his vision is, is that true Mr. Sugg?"

Ernie stood up with a sheepish grin on his face and said, "Well Johnny it was all a matter of simple mathematics. First somebody said that you said that we needed a place to train young people. So, some of us started talking and somebody said I got a big piece of property that I ain't using, and then the next guy says I got kind of a construction company, but no materials, and then up steps the next one and says, well I got the money to buy the materials, but we don't know what Johnny wants, so somebody else says let's ask Johnny what he wants." Ernie leaned over toward Johnny with an outstretched hand with a cold cola in it and said, "What do you want Boss?"

Johnny took the cola, opened it and started laughing, not giggling, but belly laughing and it was contagious. Victor and Kerttu were sitting side by side and couldn't contain themselves.

"I tink we put one over on da troll from below da bridge eh," Victor said smiling around the table.

Johnny took a deep pull on the can of pop and wiped his mouth with the back of his hand as everyone settled down.

"Do you know why I'm so happy?" Johnny asked looking around at his friends. "Cause He's here, and if you can feel the presence of God around this table, than you are definitely in the right place. I know a man who left this place six months ago who thought he was in charge of something. A few weeks ago he retuned worrying whether he would even be accepted or worse whether he had anything to offer. And today he is surrounded by God's mighty army. Brothers and sisters there ain't nothin we can't do," he shouted.

"All this talking is making me hungry," Paul said. "This banjo picker promised a free lunch if we followed him. Well, we followed him and now we're going to follow him back the Ojibwa Casino where one of you high rollers is going to stand at the end of the buffet line and pick up the tab."

"I guess dat'll be me," said Victor with a smile.

The meeting was immediately moved to a pre arranged banquet table in the casino. All were seated as Johnny rose from the head of the table, and asked everyone to bow their heads.

> "*Father God,* he began, *it is only fitting and proper that You most of all be welcomed to our celebration for you are the reason for our very being. We thank You for bringing us together to help do your mighty work. Around our area we see so many things that through your benevolence can be so much better. Father the greatest gift you have given us is our joy in fellowship to do your will. Take these many hands and many skills and lead us to a better place. Bless the hands that*

*have prepared this meal to bolster our lives
in service to You, Amen."*

As the luncheon was slowing down, Ernie and a young
man came up and sat next to Johnny. By this time Johnny
had a chance to reflect on what just happened and was just
enjoying the atmosphere.

"Johnny, this is Barry Fox, one of my older foster kids;
one of the smart ones."

"It's a pleasure to meet you Barry."

"Barry is a graduate of the University of Michigan's
Taubman College of Architectural design. Did I get that
right?" Ernie asked Barry.

"Ya Pops, you still got it," Barry responded. "What Pop's
is trying to say is that I have my own firm in Marquette that
builds stuff. I helped out on the Youth Mission plans and
when this training center came up it seemed like a natural
fit for what my firm does."

"He didn't mention the cost, cause there isn't any" Ernie
said with a smile.

"That's very generous of both of you, and I accept. Barry
one of our youth died in a car accident recently and we are
having a Memorial Service the Saturday after Labor Day.
After that our schedule should be lighter and we will have
had time to assess what our needs will be. I'll have my
favorite builder stay in touch and we can meet in the middle
of September to begin planning for the future. Thank
you Barry and you too Ernie for all you do," Johnny said
escorting them out the door. Johnny stood by the entrance
of the casino and thanked every individual who was part of
the plan. There were some he didn't know, and that made
it even more special.

CHAPTER 22

The lake trout were running out of Bete Grise on Lake Superior during the Labor Day weekend, and for a lot of folks that took precedence over work anytime. The Keweenaw Peninsula is shaped like a shark with its mouth facing east. That mouth is a half mile of sandy beach. Years ago the Corp of Engineers divided that beach and built a channel for a Port of Peril into Lac La Belle for ships experiencing rough weather on Superior. That sandy shore line was also a spawning ground for the trout and salmon which come from the deep water and spawn in the fall. R.J.'s dad was a master fisherman and when Ernie asked R.J. if maybe his dad could harvest a few of the tasty fish, Robert jumped at the chance to feel needed.

"Now dee's ain't da big fatties dat every body catches," Robert said leaning on the back of his rusted old pick-up truck sitting in Ernie's driveway. "Dee's are da smaller tastier ones. Da ones da Hackala family always eats."

Ernie was amazed that the pesky flies had ridden all the way from the harbor in Lac La Belle on the backs of these beautiful fish. He hoped they would return with Robert when he left. R.J. and his dad shook hands and said that they would have to get together soon. As infrequently as they met, that invitation never seemed to happen.

"Now careful with the fridge and the fish caldron" said Brenda.

Del and R.J. were dragging the Beer Fridge, and Ernie and Juan were hefting the fish boil cauldron out to the grassless part of the back yard. Like many events in the lives of the Sugg family, the barrel of beer and the lake trout boil was an annual event. Ernie vaguely remembered inheriting the cast iron cauldron with the reinforced stand and the two aluminum baskets from one of his sisters but couldn't remember which one. A pile of mixed hardwood was stacked on sight to provide the heat for the boil. There was also a quarter barrel of beer in the fridge with a handy spigot through the door plus a relatively new creation; the red plastic cup.

Sometime early in the evening, people began arriving with bags of small redskin potatoes and Spanish onions to go in the boil. Pies, cakes, homemade breads and salads were all part of the ticket to enjoy the evening. It was always a privilege to light and maintain the fire, and this year R.J., Del, and Juan shared the honor.

A couple of neighbor ladies gutted and cleaned the fish chopping them into chunks. Ernie was sitting on a bench drinking a beer admiring all of the busy work that was going on around him.

Brenda came down the back steps and the fall ritual began. Eva was walking next to her carrying the spice bags filled with Bay Leaf, All Spice, and pepper corns. Ernie got up, poured Brenda a beer and together they watched the boys light the fire.

For a successful fish boil the cauldron is filled with twenty gallons of water and brought to a boil. When the water is ready three pounds of salt and the spice bag are added followed by the first basket of red skin potatoes. Ten minutes later the onions are added for a few more minutes and then more salt and finally the basket of fish. Ten minutes later the fish are flaky and the meal is done. The top of the water is skimmed to remove any unpleasantness and wooden poles are strung through the handles and the fish and steaming vegetables are carried to the table where willing hands serve up the meal. The baskets are cooled with a hose and refilled with more fish and veggies and the ritual is started again. The people who missed the first batch are in charge of the second, so the tasty assembly line keeps moving until everyone has had their fill. Forty five minutes later the participants of the annual fish boil were stuffed.

"I'm thinking that a piece of Thimbleberry pie might hit the spot," Ernie said to no one in particular. "I'm thinking if you've got the energy to fetch it, you can bring me one too," said Brenda stretching out in a lawn chair. Nobody moved.

Over on the other side of the back yard, R.J. and Eva challenged Del and Fiona to a game of horse shoes. Juan was pushing Juanita on a swing set that Ernie had built a long time ago for his previous army of foster kids.

"I'm thinking that R.J. and Eva are a little friendlier than they were a week ago," Ernie observed.

"Must be the weather," remarked Brenda.

"Maybe we better keep an eye on the weather eh."

⚶

Houghton and Hancock were both bustling with all of the students returning for fall semester at Michigan Tech and Finlandia University. The stores and restaurants were happy to see the kids back in town with smiling faces and their credit cards. Johnny's parents called on Saturday to make sure their reservations were confirmed for the following weekend at the Hancock Motel.

"Can you handle the rooms, or should I call Jenny?" Angie asked.

"Just a minute you can ask her yourself," he said.

"Hello mom," Jenny said. "It's good to hear your voice."

"Mom," Angie said. "You know honey that's the nicest thing anybody has called me in a long time."

"Well, it's nothing official, but this preacher's kid keeps hinting around."

"That would make us all very happy," Angie said. "Meanwhile we want to make sure we have two rooms reserved for next weekend."

"Ground floor by the Lake near the pool," Jenny confirmed.

"Perfect," Angie said. "See you on Friday."

"Your mom said good bye," Jenny said sitting on Johnny's lap in one of the big recliners in the back corner of the Mission.

"Did I hear you mention that someone was thinking about getting married?"

"I don't remember any specific information, but it's not a subject that hasn't been kicked around before; at least a little bit," she said.

"Well, would you like to kick it around a little bit more," Johnny teased.

"That depends, on who you're talking about," she said laying her head on his shoulder.

"Jenny will you marry me?" He asked.

"Yes," she said, "But not too soon."

They kissed deeply.

"Did you just propose to me?" She asked sitting up looking him in the face.

"Jenny will you marry me? I think I just asked twice."

"I love you more than anybody on earth," she said.

"Huh."

∽

Traffic at the Mission picked up with both high school students as well as collegians checking it out. Paul was back running the day shift with Del and Johnny sharing the afternoon and after dinner crowd. Mutual respect was the biggest problem. Freshman and sophomore male students from the colleges felt a sense of entitlement while senior high school girls were throwing themselves at the Techies. More than once Del had to man the ship while Johnny took the young abusers for a walk around the block to discuss bullying versus fair play, and the joy of camaraderie. Usually the conversations ended with a high five, but occasionally an ejection was needed if only for a cooling off period.

The majority of the kids always protected and respected the rules at the Mission and everyone had fun. On Wednesday morning Johnny scheduled a meeting to finalize the plans for the Bob Rogers Memorial on Saturday.

"You know Bertha might be the smartest person I've ever met," said Lakeesha. "I mean she must know every person in the area, and not only that, she asks and everybody donates. I've never seen anything like it."

"I think they just call it Yooper know how," Bertha said.

Being lauded by a college student was a new experience for her.

Becky and Rod had also gone begging and the Kaleva Bakery was donating a catered breakfast for Friday Morning.

Paul and Johnny had been working on the program regarding speeches and dedications. J.D. and his buddies were taking the van for a wash and wax job on Thursday in preparation for picking up the family. "Some of the girls had been working on a sign to hang over the Soda Bar which said "Bob's Soda Bar". It seemed kind of sappy to some of the guys, but the ladies insisted; so it would hang. A picture of Bob goofing off by the ping pong table had been discovered, enlarged and mounted on the wall to the delight of everyone. A recording of The Star Spangled Banner and, O Canada had been found to give the opening a little international flavor. Del had volunteered to play both anthems at the same time on his banjo, but that idea was nixed and Del was ordered to get soft drinks for the entire team. A proclamation had been drawn up and signed by all the team members to be presented by Lakeesha to the Rogers family.

"Don't you think that maybe we're over doing it a little bit," said Chuck pulling a Tech hockey hat down over his face.

"Exactly," said Johnny. "Isn't it fun?"

The team just looked at each other and grinned. J.D leaned over and gave Chuck a cuff on the back of his head.

CHAPTER 23

On Friday morning the shiny van pulled up in front of the Mission and J.D. jumped out of the driver's seat and ran around the van to open the doors. Johnny and Paul smiled at each other, both noticing J.D. was a little out of uniform wearing a new shirt and tie.

"Good Morning," Johnny said shaking hands with Rob and Ruth. "I'm Johnny Hendricks, and this is Paul Rader, our Mission Director. Welcome to the Hancock Youth Mission."

Ruth introduced George and Grace while the young men from Tech made sure to shake hands with Grace, a seventeen year old daughter who was older and prettier than expected. All of the young men looked at Chuck as if he had been holding out on them, but he just shrugged his shoulders and feigned innocence.

"I've got name tags for everyone up in our breakfast room so let's all go in and get acquainted," Johnny said.

The Roger's family was impressed by the quaintness of the Houghton-Hancock area, and when they entered the Mission they were amazed at the way the main floor was arranged. They smiled politely at the Committee personnel as they looked at the game area as well as the study and socializing areas.

The aroma of the Pulla Coffee Bread made by Brenda from her grandma's old Finnish recipe came wafting down the stairs inviting the guests to come up. Becky and Rod had outdone themselves with the breakfast plan, and with help from Kaleva's kitchen staff, the guests were delighted. With the table set for sixteen, Johnny asked everyone to take a seat. Johnny and Paul sat at the ends of the table with the Rob and Ruth on either side of Johnny while George and Grace sat with the Techies. Johnny stood and everyone sat quietly.

"Please allow me to ask our Father to bless this meal."

"Father God we welcome you this morning to join us in nourishing our bodies as well as creating a new friendship with our brother Bob's family. We honor him this weekend for all that he did to help create the joy and the youthful flavor of our organization. He was certainly one of our bright stars as a youth leader, and is missed every day. Bless the many hands that helped to prepare this feast before us to strengthen our bodies so that we might do Your good works, Amen."

"That was the most beautiful prayer I have ever heard," Ruth said smiling at Johnny through tearful eyes.

After the eggs, bacon, sausage and thick slices of the warm cardamom Pulla bread slathered with Thimbleberry jam, nobody wanted to move. The teens went downstairs to play foosball and ping pong while the adults had another cup of coffee.

"That may well have been the best breakfast I've ever had," said Rob loosening his belt. "I notice a distinctive

Finnish flavor in the two cities. Were they the original settlers?"

"I'd like to answer that," said Bob Heikinen. "The modern day discovery of copper all around the Peninsula in the late 1840's drew people from all over. The social system's of Europe didn't offer much to the lower class citizenry, so adventurers from Wales, Finland, Poland, Italy and many other lands jumped on ships and sailed to New York. Finding that the northern Great Lakes were similar to Finland they headed for the U.P. where the logging and mining industries were beginning to flourish. It was a physically hard way of life for the Finns, but no more difficult than what they were used to. Everyone wrote home and sent money to bring their families to America, and within a couple of generations a new Finnish/American culture was born. I'm sure that this blending of cultures with each new group of immigrants happened all over North America, including your great nation," he said to Rob.

"Those really must have been exciting times for the new comers, but I'm not sure I'd have wanted to be a wife or a mother living in those days," Ruth said.

"Some went back, but many more came, and when the need for copper exploded, they found themselves in a new middle class and were grateful," added Bob.

The conversation dwindled and the Kaleva caterers began their clean up.

"In an hour, two high school busses will line up in front of the Mission to offer rides to anyone wishing to join us for the wreath laying. I hope you don't mind, but when the students at Tech heard the story about Bob, many wanted to be a part of it. The local police will provide an escort to the sight and make sure everyone is safe.

Ruth smiled, stood and hugged her husband. She leaned

over and kissed Johnny on the cheek but her daughter surrounded by several young men didn't notice.

In spite of the air temperature, there was a cold breeze blowing from the North West that made many wish they had brought a sweater. Johnny hadn't realized how narrow the roadway was where the accident occurred, but the Michigan State Police had barricaded the south bound lane with road blocks. The school buses pulled up to the scene of the accident, allowed the mourners to exit the vehicles, and then proceed to a wider parking area. Johnny's van pulled up to a boulder overlooking the accident scene and he, Paul, Chuck and the family were a little hesitant about climbing out into the blustery air. Johnny glanced down over the edge but there was no evidence of the horror that had occurred there. It was the first time he had visited the scene and wondered whether Rod was experiencing the same feelings. A police officer led Lakeesha, Becky, Rod, Heather, Miia, and Jenny through the crowd up to join Johnny and the family. Paul walked back to the Van and collected the wreath. A portable sound system was set up and the fifty or so people squeezed to one side of the road as the State Police using radios allowed north and south bound traffic to alternately proceed in the outside lane.

Θ》

"Can everyone hear me?" said Johnny into the microphone. People in the back row nodded their heads. At the last second Johnny noticed that a police officer was escorting Del and Fiona toward the front with instruments in hand.

"Jesus said I am the Resurrection and the Life. He that

believeth in me though he were dead, yet shall he live, and whosoever liveth and believeth in Me shall never die. For we know that if our earthly house were dissolved, we have a building of God, a house not made by man, but one eternal in the heavens," quoted Johnny from the Bible. Today we gather on the edge of this highway to honor the memory of a child of God who brought a lot of joy to friends and family here on this earth. We raise up the name of Robert Charles Rogers Jr., beloved son of Robert Charles, mother Ruth Ward Rogers, and brother to George and Grace. Those who knew him and loved him requested this song."

Del and Fiona stood up against the boulder away from the wind and sang. *Some glad morning when this life is over I'll fly awayTo a home on God's celestial shore, I'll fly away.*

Amazingly most of the both young and old joined the chorus.

I'll fly away o glory, I'll fly away
When I die hallelujah by and by I'll fly away.

Suddenly the freezing temperature which had brought discomfort only moments ago seemed to disappear as Del and Fiona smiled and played an instrumental chorus between verses.

When the shadows of this life have grown, I'll fly away

People were clapping their hands and tiny children were doing circles around their mother's extended fingers. One twenty something man with a long beard and Bermuda shorts with matching socks was dancing with a little boy in his arms in the back of the crowd with a police officer trying to protect them from the traffic. The passing vehicles took turns stopping wondering what was going on. When Del hung a bluegrass ending on the tune, the crowd roared. It truly was a celebration of Bob's old life and his new one with God.

"I'd like to introduce Bob's best friend Chuck Atkins from Toronto, Canada."

"Whoever you are or where ever you're from, we, the family of Bob and me thank you so much for coming because you have caught the spirit of this fun-loving man. The night before he passed, we were sitting around the house talking and he told me that he had found something and some people who had really touched his heart. He realized that he was not an academic, but some one who earnestly wanted to make things better for others. It sounds kind of sappy but I think maybe God took him up for more training. Anyway I'd like to thank you all for being part of this. It's really special."

He stepped away from the microphone and Ruth gave him a big hug.

"I'm going to ask all of the people who were in the van that fateful afternoon to make their way down to the big stone in the middle of the hill along with Chuck carrying the wreath."

Chuck went first followed by Paul Rader who walked backwards guiding the youngsters. Miia and Lakeesha came down the hill together and put their arms around each other. Jenny walked up to the microphone and put her arm around Johnny and hugged him as he leaned forward.

> *"Father God, in times like these when there don't seem to be any answers that make sense to us we turn to You. In spite of the sorrow we feel for the loss of our friend, we are grateful that You will help see us through the darkness. We can't claim to know why, but we know that You will bring us into the light accepting our mortality, and realizing that we are only passing through toward*

*eternal life. Help us to take the few moments
of time we have spent with Bob, and to learn
from his goodness and joy to become better
persons through You Lord, Amen."*

Fiona played the introduction to *Amazing Grace* and Del joined in on the banjo as she sang all verses in her lilting Irish voice.

"To all of you who took the time from your busy fall schedules, we are grateful for your presence. On behalf of the Rogers family…"

"Wait a minute," Rob said grabbing the Mic. "My family and I would like to invite all of you, including you wonderful policemen, for dinner at the Youth Mission in Hancock at 6 P.M. absolutely free. Come as you are because my wife and I would like to meet every one of you. Please come," he added again and jocularly handed the Mic. back to Johnny.

"You don't get many invitations like that every day," said Johnny, "at least not up here in the Keweenaw."

Johnny signaled for Del and Fiona, and as the survivors took pictures of each other by the wreath, the pickers from North Ireland and Eastern Kentucky flew right into *I Saw the Light.* Hank Williams would have been proud of the joy his song had brought to more than sixty singing, hand clapping, and dancing strangers celebrating the life of one young Canadian named Robert Charles Rogers Jr.

CHAPTER 24

The sky was over cast as the sun began to burn off the fog covering Portage Lake on the Saturday morning of the Memorial. Bertha was on the phone at 6 A.M. calling all of the Youth Mission kids who had foolishly given her their number. Marine Drill sergeants had nothing on Bertha when she was on a mission, and Johnny was no exception.

"Do you think this place is going to clean itself," she said with as much moxie as she could muster.

"Ah, who is this?" Johnny muttered with only one eye open.

"This is your worst nightmare," she grumbled, "and if you're not here in 15 minutes to clean this place up, I'll have everybody you were entertaining last night knocking on your front door." Click.

Twelve minutes later, with an old sweatshirt, cut offs and flip flops on, Johnny ran through the front door of the Mission. There were already at least twenty people running around trying to keep out of Bertha's way. Johnny grabbed a push broom and headed up stairs.

"Not so fast, Party Boy," she said standing at the bottom of the steps. "There will be a meeting in ten minutes in the kitchen to see if we've got this thing together," she said menacingly.

"We've got the draped banner," Paul said pointing to the sign over the snack bar. "I've given the Proclamation to Lakeesha to present to the family. J.D. has the recorder cued up for the National Anthems. So why does it take so long to make the coffee," he whimpered.

"Perhaps if the Director of the Youth Mission had gotten here a little bit earlier," said Bertha coming through the kitchen door. Once again she had everyone's attention. "I have my final list, and all I want to hear are "Yes's"

"1. Valet or help for people parking."

"Yes," said young male voice.

"2. Sound System."

"Yes," said J.D.

"3. Escort for family and corsages for mother and daughter including pins and steady hands."

"Yes," said Heather with confidence.

"4. Ushers."

"Yes," said a deep voice. "Six in all."

"5. Finger foods and drinks."

"Yes," said Becky, "All from Kaleva."

"It is an honor and privilege to work with such a competent group," Bertha said. "Oh I just noticed the coffee pot light go on. Please see that the Director gets the first cup," she said as she exited the kitchen with clip board in hand.

"Wow," Chuck said to no one in particular. We're all set and we only have three and a half hours to wait. I'm thinking a nap."

At 10:30 everyone was back at the Mission and nervously pacing the floor. The Mining Gazette News Paper was setting up shots for the front page photos on Monday and reporters were interviewing anybody who would talk. Everyone who was involved was either at their stations or rehearsing what they had to say. Johnny was sitting with his folks and Dutch, as well as Jenny and Helen in their favorite corner on the ground floor reminiscing about their mini vacation the previous Thanksgiving.

"It sure seems like a long time ago," said Helen.

"Well, we can't say it was boring," Angie said smiling at her son. Johnny sat fidgeting with his watch.

"I know you're not concerned about the events this morning," his dad said.

"Folks who have been through as much as we have to get to this day certainly realize that God has everything in hand," Dutch said.

"Here comes the white van," someone hollered, and Johnny jumped to his feet and rushed to the front door almost knocking over a lamp.

CHAPTER 25

"Lady's and gentlemen, will you please rise for the National Anthems of Canada and the United States." A recorded drum roll ensued and everyone stood and faced the Maple Leaf Flag.

The upstairs performance room was packed to capacity and extra audio speakers were placed down stairs to facilitate the overflow. The stage had been expanded to seat all of the dignitaries who were invited. Johnny, Paul, and Bob Heikinen were seated in the center. Flanking Bob were Howard Berg, the President of the Historical Society, Winfred Mann, The Dean of Michigan Tech., and Virna Warala, Dean of Finlandia University. Flanking Paul were Johnny's father and Grandfather, representing their churches, Keith Alton, Mayor of Houghton and Father Walter, Leader of the Houghton/Hancock Clergy Association. Standing in the middle of the front row with their hands over their hearts were the Rogers Family, and behind them were more than a hundred friends, relatives and mostly curious citizens who wondered what the fuss was about.

The Star Spangled Banner followed O Canada, and some even sang the lyrics.

Johnny then asked Father Walter to open with a prayer, and with a loud resonant "Amen" everyone took their seats.

Johnny held the podium with both hands and began. "It is an honor and a privilege to be standing here in front of you today to help remember a fallen brother. In fact it is an honor and a privilege to be standing anywhere, because as most of you know, the accident that took our friend Bob Rogers deprived me of the use of my legs for six months. I don't tell you these facts for sympathy or concern. I mention them this morning to show you that good things can come from tragedy, and we can all learn from these disastrous events and go forward to try and make this world a better place. That is why we are all here this morning.

Our guests of honor are Robert and Ruth Rogers and their children George and Grace, who drove from Toronto a couple of days ago, to help us celebrate the life of their son. Behind me you will notice the 'cream of the crop' of our two cities. Represented this morning are our two Universities, the Mayor of Houghton, the City Council President of Hancock, The President of our Local Historical Society, the head of the Clergy Association, and finally my dad and my grandpa, both Pastors from Grand Rapids, who are primarily responsible for all of us being here this morning. I would like to have them all stand and introduce themselves, but we have only rented this hall for an hour."

The crowd all laughed and applauded.

"What cannot be lost in their collective presence is the importance that this august body places on the youth of this area, and their eagerness to get involved. I would like us all to give them a warm welcome."

The audience stood and applauded.

"Now I would like to introduce the Director of the Hancock City Youth Mission, Mr. Paul Rader."

Once again there was thunderous applause as well as a few hoots and hollers from the youth in the back.

As Paul walked to the podium, it surprised a number of his ex students and teacher friends, how much more confident and out going he had become.

"Thank you Johnny," he said, "and thank you all for coming. To those who drive by the Mission every day and wonder what's going on in here, take a good look around. A year ago when you drove by, all you could see were dirty windows reflecting an unconcerned community. Then Johnny came, and somebody washed the windows and turned the lights on. Those weren't the lights in the old appliance store, those were the lights inside of our heads which said it's time for a new idea. It's time to invest in ourselves, not only in money but in love and a new way of thinking. I would like to introduce to you someone who didn't grow up here, but saw the possibilities of a derelict old building, and derelict old ideas rising to new heights. Please welcome our youth leader Lakeesha Johnson, a sophomore from Michigan Tech."

As Lakeesha walked up the steps, an easel with a cloth draped over a frame was carried up the other side of the stage.

"As Paul said, my name is Lakeesha Johnsoninen, and I'm from just south of Portage Lake from a little town called Detroit." Lakesha had charmed the locals and they reacted with a titter.

"If you are unfamiliar with the name Detroit, it comes from an old Indian word meaning "Can't beat the Packers."

The place went nuts.

"It's good to laugh," she said, "better yet it's good to have a place to laugh, a place to talk, a place to share idea and learn from each other. Plus, it's a good place to check out the guys; right ladies?"

There were a few snickers from the girls.

"But mostly it is a good place to make a stand; to offer up a truth, and declare a conviction. Can I have the Rogers family come forward please?"

The four Canadians made their way up the steps and accepted a standing ovation. The drape was lowered from the easel and Lakeesha read, *The Hancock Youth Mission Council has unanimously declared that every second Saturday in September henceforth will be Bob Rogers Day. Those officers of the council will endeavor to provide some form of entertainment on or around this date to honor the joyous spirit provided by our own Bob Rogers who represented the very best of good will and positive thinking.*

Everyone stood and celebrated Bob's memory. Bob's dad and the rest of the grateful family circled the Podium.

Clearing his throat and acknowledging a few people he had met the night before Rob said,

"Hi, for those of you that we didn't meet last night, I'm Rob. When you bring children into this world, you take what the Lord gives you and try to do the best you can. I think that might be the perfect definition of parenthood. If it's a son you hope he is smart, handsome, and strong," he paused looking for reassurance from Ruth, "but you take what you get. You love them and hope for the best. Well our son wasn't really any of those things, and many nights Ruth and I would try and figure out what he might become."

There wasn't a sound in the room as this father poured out his heart to an auditorium full of strangers. Rob stopped and scratched the back of his head.

"You know I had to drive to a foreign country to find out that our oldest son, Bobby, was loved by more people than I probably know. And, without counsel from his old man, he decided that his heart and future was in helping people like you. That is a humbling and a blessed feeling at the same time. I'm gonna let Ruth talk now," he said.

Rob assisted by his son and daughter was helped back to his seat while Ruth remained at the microphone.

"As a little surprise and a way of thanking all of you good people, our family has been working with administrators from Michigan Tech, and Finlandia U., and we would like to announce today that starting next fall we will provide two full scholarships, one to each University, as part of a trust called the Robert Charles Rogers Jr. Scholarship Fund. God has truly blessed us with a successful business and three wonderful children, and we would like to share our blessings with those around us. Thank you."

Ruth and Rob smiled at each other during the applause, and then she quietly returned to her seat.

Paul Rader returned to the Podium shaking his head.

"I'm not quite sure what to say after that generous gift except thank you. I believe our friend Johnny has one more item on the agenda."

Johnny, who had been standing off to the side, walked up to his dad and grandpa and shook their hands on the way to the podium. He waited until all was quiet and began.

"It was about eleven months ago, in mid October, that I crossed the blue Portage Lake Lift Bridge for the first time and entered into a new life. I was inexperienced, cocky, and filled with enthusiasm as I inadvertently set forth to turn this beautiful little city upside down. My hopes were clear but my approach was flawed. I offended people that I would learn to know and love, and I forgot the first rule in building relationships. I didn't listen. An angel from God by the name of Helen Aho, one of your neighbors, sat me down on a kitchen chair and through love and wisdom began tutoring me with simple logic and mutual respect."

Johnny winked at Helen who was sitting in the second row next to Jenny.

"With a new attitude, I learned that civic leaders like Bob Heikinen, and Howard Berg were not against me, but for Hancock, and all of its citizens. And then God laid his mighty hand on all of us. We became a team. People with unique talents were suddenly at our sides offering their innate gifts to help grease the wheels and smooth the path toward this magnificent facility we sit in today. We experienced a local household catastrophe only to see it turned into the rebirth of one of our finest families in the area. We also experienced a tragedy which left us drained and could have halted all our hard work, but God had another lesson for us in the form of a cool young Canadian, our friend Bob Rogers. In many ways he was a lot like me back in October. Confident in what he wanted, but unsure of how to do it. He and his friend Chuck Atkins came to the Keweenaw to find success, and instead helped create a success without even knowing it. These two freshmen stood back to back to protect each other from the anxieties of a new culture, but instead spread their easy going way of doing things where ever they went. The night before he died, Bob confided in his friend that he had found a new path after being named as an officer in the Youth Council the night before. The false bravado was gone. The truth was that he was going to commit his life to working for others. He wasn't with us long enough to realize what his true calling might be, or where it would take him, but on that Saturday he was a new man. That new man was taken before he could put his thumb print on the future, but his joy and inspiration has lifted us all up, and by the Proclamation his memory will go on.

Johnny raised his right hand.

"Father God, You continue to make new disciples to help us find our way. We thank you for giving us Bob as a beacon to help light our path to do your will, Amen."

Johnny caught Kerttu and Halle's eyes at the other end of the second row.

"The Dictionary defines the word miracle as an extraordinary event manifesting divine intervention in human affairs," he continued. "What we have all tried to say in our own ways this morning meet that criterion. But where does the miracle end? When do we say now we are done?" Johnny asked looking around. "The answer to this miracle is not yet my friends. While languishing in my own self pity a month ago, God offered a new challenge in the form of a couple of teenagers who were lost. They were not lost in the physical sense, but in the sense that time had past them by, and they felt they had nothing to offer or contribute to the world. It was all around me and I hadn't noticed. I had thought that by helping build this Mission we could provide a future in terms of intellectual camaraderie and positive relationships, and I still believe that to be true. Unfortunately there are far too many of our youth who weren't properly motivated or offered the right opportunities according to their abilities. They quietly stepped aside from the challenge and became dreamers who worshipped rock stars and athletes. The commercial world made it easier by propping up teen heroes and solidifying their positions by movies and video games to reinforce their mediocrity."

People in the seats weren't sure where this was going, or whether they really wanted to know.

"One night recently, that still small voice said that it was time to go back and pick up the ones we left behind. The vision came in the form of a training center; a place where someone who could do something practical could teach you to do the same thing.

Just west of Baraga off of Highway 38, twenty acres of land is being cleared for this purpose. Next week, plans will be drawn up for a multi-room facility to address this over sight. Money from some generous fellow citizens has been graciously donated to build this state of the art work shop. You notice I didn't say school, because that word has become a negative symbol to many of those who have failed, or better yet, those youths who have not yet achieved. The next question you may ask is how does that affect me, or what can I do to help. We don't know yet. We will figure that out in the next weeks and months and when we do I hope that you will all be a part of it. I'm sure that many of the folks sitting behind me who represent so much of where we live will give us wise counsel as we move forward. I'd now like to turn it back over to our Mission leader Paul."

CHAPTER 26

EPILOGUE
(Twenty Years Later)

"Traelo aqui, por favor," shouted Angie.

"Si abuela," replied Mary Helen, her granddaughter, as the nine year old slogged through the beach sand and plopped down right next to Papa John with a fist full of mail.

Papa John wasn't necessarily against bilingualism. He just thought that at the ripe old age of sixty-seven, Papa John sounded better than Abuelo Jose.

The incoming mail was always on time in Mazatlan, Mexico, no matter what time it came. The Hendricks' decided that after retirement it was finally time to see where Angelina really came from. With a lifetime of connections with government agencies, it wasn't too hard for John to track down her cousins in the state of Sinaloa on the Mazatlan coast. A couple of years before retirement, she confided to John that she would like to visit her old home and see if there was something she could do to get closer to her family. She wrote letters to her cousins and they said come on down.

They flew down for a two week vacation and loved the area, especially the sun and the beach.

When John finally hung up his robe, they made sure that Dutch was okay and well situated. A young pastoral foreign exchange student from the Netherlands was looking for lodging while at Calvin College so they moved him in with Dutch for the school year.

Angie's cousin found them a place to rent near the beach, and so they began their new adventure.

Everything seemed to be working out fine. She started tutoring English to a number of Mexican teenagers, and John was working on his memoirs, as well as learning how to surf fish from one of Angie's nephews.

"Anything for me," John asked as Angie was sorting through the Christmas cards from Michigan.

"There must be something here for you," she said smiling at Johnny's daughter Mary Helen. Johnny and Jenny had started a tradition of flying down with the kids for the Christmas holidays. Their son John Paul the 4th, (J.P.) was twelve years old and starting middle school so the holidays were a good time for him to come. He was in his second year of Spanish at school in Hancock and beginning to notice the senoritas, so another great opportunity afforded itself.

Johnny came strolling down the beach with a cooler full of soft drinks and another beach umbrella. "Que Pasa," he said to no one in particular and opened the cooler. J.P. and a couple of distant relatives his age were right behind Johnny kicking a soccer ball. The boys took a quick right and raced each other into the blue waters of the Pacific Ocean.

"Ah, here's one from Bertha Mittala." Angie said handing it to Jenny. The card was a picture of the Hancock City Hall with a wreath on the door and snow falling.

"She says 'Hauskaa Joulua, (Merry Christmas) from the

Mayor/Council President and family," Jenny read aloud.
"It seems so long ago that we were all together growing the
Mission. We had our annual Advent Dinner at Helens last
night, and missed you all. Bob and Judy Heikenin were there
and are packing for Bermuda, and Howard and Maggie are
in Florida all ready. They say they'll miss the snow, but I
doubt it. (Ha Ha)

Ernie and Brenda invited Halle Lehtoe to join us this
year. He is writing a book about the old days and of course
Kerttu is the star. He said she would have been one hundred
and twenty this year. I can still picture her saying how good
she looks for that age.

Tell your folks that R.J. and Eva are expecting their
fourth child in August. R.J. is hoping for a boy this time.
Juanita says Hello.

We tried to get Victor Wurtz to join us last night, but he
won't leave that new puppy alone in the house. I think they
are probably training each other.

We're all looking forward to seeing you in January.
P.S. Say Hi to the folks.
Love Bertha"

"Here's one from Keith and Mary in Rockford," Angie
announced to the family. "A post card with a picture of their
daughter Amy Lynn age (22), and son William Richard (18)
leaning against the railing at Peppler Park on a beautiful
fall day.

Best wishes for a blessed holiday season," she read.
"We're looking forward to working with you both at the
Keweenaw Training Center this July. I've got some ideas for
a CPR class.

Say Hi to mom and dad.
Love Keith and Mary"

"And finally the last one is for dad from Paul Rader," Mary Helen said stomping around the beach umbrella and handing it to Johnny.

"Merry Christmas from the North Pole, or just south of it in Hancock," he writes. "We missed you all at the Annual Carol Sing lasts Sunday night. It was a great idea having a raffle for entry tickets. We still had people standing in the street below the window singing with us. I think the whole town was here. We got a Christmas card from Del and Fiona from Lough Neagh in Northern Ireland. They are performing with her sister Ann, and Ann's husband Shamus. They said they would send us a C.D.

Finally, do you remember Chuck Atkins from Toronto? He sent the Mission a C.D. of his comedy act. He's a stand-up comedian on the Canadian circuit and says he's doing well.

I'm looking forward to spending Christmas with my folks, and Jessie and Rod.

See you soon,
Paul"

The afternoon flew by much too quickly, and as the sun began to dip in the western sky, John marched all of the troops over to the fresh water shower to wash off all of the salt water and the sand. By the time they reached their little rented home on the hillside behind Mazatlan, the sun was ready to sizzle into the Pacific. Jenny got the kids into their pajamas while Johnny made a cart load of tacos and nachos. The whole family and all of Angie's cousins and children, sat around the camp fire and listened to a nephew play his guitar and sing a soft love song in Spanish that only half of the family understood.

"Praise God from whom all blessing flow," Angie whispered into her granddaughter's ear.

ABOUT THE AUTHOR

Once again, Holmes has chosen Michigan's Upper Peninsula for his third novel, *Keweenaw Faith*. His intimate knowledge of the copper country around the Keweenaw Peninsula allows him to weave a tale of challenges and ultimate successes. Holmes, a retired auto worker from the Detroit area has visited the Keweenaw for more than forty years, and it shows in his familiarity with the people and the beautiful peninsula.

Printed in the United States
By Bookmasters